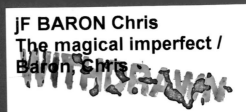

the Magical Imperfect

the Magical Imperfect

CHRIS BARON

Feiwel and Friends
New York

A FEIWEL AND FRIENDS BOOK
An imprint of Macmillan Publishing Group, LLC
120 Broadway, New York, NY 10271
mackids.com

Library of Congress Cataloging-in-Publication Data is available.

First edition, 2021
Book design by Trisha Previte
Watercolor background © vellot/Shutterstock
Printed in the United States of America by LSC Communications,
Harrisonburg, Virginia
Feiwel and Friends logo designed by Filomena Tuosto

ISBN 978-1-250-76782-0 (hardcover)
10 9 8 7 6 5 4 3 2 1

For Ella,
and our whole family here,
in the Philippines, and beyond.
Thank you for rescuing me.

Part
1

Earthquake Drill

The alarm
is a wave
that knocks us
out of our chairs.
Pencils fly,
papers float in the air,
chairs squeak
as we dive
under our desks.
But nobody is scared.
It's only a drill.

We are getting used to them.
There were a few small quakes
over the summer,
so school makes us
do drills once a week.
But I don't like how loud it gets,
the alarm's bell sound winding up
and down and up again.
We wait until
we're told
it's time to go outside.

When we get to the field,
Jordan and the other boys
argue about the World Series.
Jordan used to be my best friend
until our parents got in an argument
that broke everything into pieces,
so it's different now.
He spends his time with Martin.

Martin thinks the A's and the Giants
are going to be in it.
A's in '89, he says. *No one steals
bases like Rickey Henderson.*
If I wanted to speak up,
I would tell him no way.
Candy Maldonado is too good in the outfield.
Dad and I always root for the Giants!

Speak

When we come back
to class, we have
to finish our quiz
by reciting five helping verbs.
Except I don't have to;
I have a note that
says it's okay for me
to write things down.
I don't like to speak
in front of people.
Some teachers say I won't.
But it's not that.
I don't like to talk.

My father says
it's because my mom had to go.
The doctor he takes me to
agrees with him
and thinks it may be "selective mutism."
But I don't have anyone
I *want* to talk to right now.

I'd rather spend time on Main Street
with my grandfather in his jewelry shop,
where he fixes broken things
and makes them whole again.

Sometimes I watch my father build houses.
He can hammer a nail in with one swing.
Not me. I'm kind of small,
and a little round,
and I can draw a tree faster
than I can hammer a nail,
so I stick to that.

Mom

I wasn't quiet before.
I liked to talk,
especially after Little League games;
Mom would take us to get ice cream,
double scoops of Rocky Road.
When we lost, she let me get a triple scoop,
which always made me feel better.
It wasn't the ice cream, it was the way
I could talk to her about everything.
It's like the ice cream was
made of magic;
it let the words drift out of me.
Words about how hard
math homework is.
Words about the way
that sometimes
the boys on the playground
told Cole that he wasn't really a boy.
We talked about cartoons and toy soldiers.
I showed her my drawings,
and she asked so many questions.

She looked and listened
with her whole body.

I guess
I should have been listening
more to her.
     I didn't know about
         her problems inside.

When she left,
I felt like part of my voice
went with her.

It's been three months since we took
her past the Golden Gate Bridge,
up and down
the roller-coaster hills
to what she says is the city's heart,
to the hospital.

> Big trees in the garden,
> roses planted in a circle
> around a fountain
> where I threw in every penny I had.

She can talk to us on the phone,
but we can only visit her once a month.
It's part of her treatment.
She tells me that she's sick
on the inside.

She says that the roads
her thoughts take
are too windy for now,
and she needs help
straightening them out.
She told me the best thing I can do
is pray for her,
take care of my dad,
> spend time with my grandfather
> until she gets back.

When she reached down
to say goodbye one last time,
she said, *I love you, Etan,*
just like when she used to tuck me in
after she finished a story.
But when I opened my mouth
to say it back,
no words
came out.

After School

After school I go down to Main Street.
It has the oldest shops in Ship's Haven
and even older people, who have seen all sorts of things.
Once, Mrs. Li told me that she remembers
when there were more wagons pulled by horses
than cars on the road.

Main Street is less than a mile
away from school,
and I can run pretty fast,
past the redwood park
where kids from school play baseball,
past our apartment
to where the river crosses the middle of town,
to the hill just above Main Street.
From there, when there isn't any fog,
you can even see San Francisco to the north
and the ocean far away.
My grandfather tells me how his boat sailed right past here
on its way to Angel Island,
when he first came to America,   a long, long time ago.

Dog Ears

Before I reach Main Street,
I pass our small apartment building.
Mrs. Hershkowitz, my neighbor,
leans out of her third-story window.
ETAN! she calls, *can you bring me
some roast beef from the deli?*
I look up as I run past, and nod,
but she can't see me well enough.
I have to speak, so she can hear me.
I take a deep breath and say, *Okay.*
WHAT? she yells, so I give her a thumbs-up.
THANK YOU, she yells, and goes inside,
and just then I see
the tufted white fur,
the bandit face of her dog,
standing at the window, tongue flying
in a wide doggy smile.

Main Street

Main Street feels like a festival.
The small shops have open doors
and wide windows.
Fish and long-tentacled creatures
hang from wires in one window,
colorful dragon-shaped kites fly in another.
Next door, fruits and vegetables fill silver bowls
along wooden tables,
apples and artichokes, tomatoes
and eggplants, cucumbers,
bins full of peanuts and dried mangoes,
a carnival of food and music.
A saxophone hums down the street
to the beating of a drum
and the strum of a guitar.

In the late afternoon,
it's even more crowded,
a sea of grown-ups, families,
kids from school
shopping or playing,
visiting grandparents,
and always always always
stopping at Dimitri's Candy Shop
for the crystal clear rock candy
he gives out for free
to any kid who asks.

The shop owners smile when they see me—
I've been coming to my grandfather's jewelry shop
ever since I can remember—
and I do my best to smile back,
but mostly I look toward the ground
because they might ask me a question,
and I don't really want to answer.

The Bakery

There is a bakery
in one of the oldest parts
of Main Street,
down a small alleyway,
where the road is brick
and letters curl into stone
with the initials of all the people
from the *Calypso*,
the ship that brought
so many families here
from over the sea.
My grandfather tells me
that for some,
it was the hardest thing
they ever did.
People had to leave their families,
or find a way to save them.
When they finally got here,
not everyone was welcome.
He tells me that people who go through
a voyage like that
will do anything
for each other.

When my grandpa first got here,
there were only small roads,
mostly just farmland,
and little by little they laid brick
for the streets
and opened more shops,
one at a time,
so they could remember
who they once were.

Not everyone sees the initials
or knows what they mean.
But I do:
different letters and characters,
even a painted flower,
like a stone garden
planted for them
to always remember
when their time here began.
I know I've arrived when I smell
fresh coffee cake,
strawberries simmering;
see cookie dough rolled out
on long, flour-sprinkled tables,
chocolate-raisin babka,
and coconut macaroons.
I stare through the front glass case.
Mr. Cohen puts his towel
over his shoulder, smiles,
and hands me a chocolate rugelach
on a napkin,
        and I sit.

I wait for him to pull the last bagels
from the boiling water.
I get one salt bagel
and one black coffee
for my grandfather,
and a soft maple cookie for me.

Grandfather

My grandfather is a giant man
with iron hands.
He works in his jewelry shop
from before the sun goes up
until long after it sets,
except on Friday,
when he leaves extra early
so he can be home
to light the Shabbat candles.

The candles, he says,
they make us Jews.

The Jewelry Shop

At his worktable in the front of the shop,
my grandfather hums his favorite song.
Golden trinkets hang
from long silver hooks,
and below them are a few glass cases
filled with necklaces,
bracelets, and other things
he's made. In the back:
wooden boxes stacked
full of metal sheets,
and chains of all sizes
and pegboards with tools
and coils of wire.

But today, there is another box,
one I haven't seen before.
Dark wood, painted green,
with two chains wrapped
around it, and a bulky metal lock.
The wood looks worn,
and engraved all over it
are faded Hebrew words.
I recognize a few I think,
maybe an alef and a nun,
but I haven't been going to shul
since my father stopped going.
I should know more Hebrew by now.

A candle burns low
in a dish on top of the box.

When my grandfather sees me,
he drops a heavy silver watch
onto his worktable at the back of the shop.
Etan, I've designed necklaces
for the fanciest banquets
and mezuzahs for every doorway,
but if I have to fix Mr. Newman's watch
one more time—it's over.
It's unfixable!
I understand that it belonged to his brother,
but there is just no
axle and wheel that can
make this work.

The Medal

I set his coffee on his workbench
and put the bagel jammed with cream cheese
on a napkin near a pile of metal discs.
These? he says, *they're medals*
for the Little League team;
I gotta get going with these.

When I was small,
my father asked my grandfather
to make me a medal
because I could never win anything.

Grandpa crafted it from real silver,
round and shiny,
with a boy flexing his muscles
etched at the center.

> *That's you, mensch.*
> *A real hero!*
He's the only one who's ever called me that.

Coughing

He finishes his bagel
and hands me a broom,
waves his hands around the shop,
First order of business,
and I know what to do.
He sits in his high stool
over his long workbench,
tools arranged in an order
only he understands.
        He's coughing.
He coughs more now than ever.
He says, *I'm just old,*
this is what happens.
I keep sweeping,
pull my pants up over my belly.

I walk over to the new box,
tap on the top;
it feels heavy, solid.
That? he says. I smile.
With my grandfather,
I rarely need words.
That, my boy, is a box
of priceless treasure
from a world so old
it will sound like a fairy tale to you.
That is my treasure from the Old Country.
From Prague.
It was all I could take with me.
It's been hidden away
since your father was a boy,
but I think it's time
to maybe unlock its secrets again.
Time for you to learn even more about our story.

He laughs, but it turns to a cough again.
He tries to stop coughing.
He motions with his hands,
Get me a glass of water.

The World Is Full

I pour some water.
My grandfather drinks.
He pulls another stool next to him.
Etan. He pats the stool. *Sit.*
He puts his giant hand on my head
and messes up my hair.
You remember what I told you?
I nod. I do remember.
        That he will live forever
        one way or the other,
                in this world or the next.

He takes my small hands
in his large ones
and I stare at his worn fingers.
Did you talk to anyone today?
I don't say anything. He sighs.
You've got to work on talking again.

The way he says this
is different than the way
everyone else does.
There is no anger;
his voice is like a flashlight
in the middle of the night
helping me find my way.
The world is like our shop.
So many beautiful things.
He waves his hands at
stacks of silver platters
and long gold chains,
cases of intricately carved earrings
and rings set with green jewels.

But the shop, Main Street,
the town? It's a gift.
We are lucky to be here. All of us.
But it is not the whole world!
It's only a part of it.
He looks over at his box,
then raises his finger
straight to the sky.
One of the best parts,
besides being with you,
is that I get to talk to people,
to hear about their lives.
Even Ruth Hershkowitz
though she drives me mad!
When he says this, I remember that
I need to get her the roast beef from the deli.

Hey, got anything new in your notebook?
I go to my backpack,
take out a notebook,
my mom's notebook,
the edges frayed, the pages stuffed
with notes and magazine clippings,
grocery lists, and even receipts.
But everywhere, on all the pages,
are her tiny doodles of flowers
and trees, windy roads, and sunsets.
And now, here and there
are doodles of my own,
lists, mazes, baseball stats,
and things I need to remember.

I fold the cover back
and open to a little doodle
sketched in pencil.
Oh, he says, *it's a parrot? I love it.*
Puffin, I think. It's a puffin.
We stare at my unfinished drawing,
waiting for the other to speak.

Ecosystem

I take a deep breath
and look toward the door.
My grandfather nods.
An errand for Mrs. Hershkowitz?
He looks at me for a long time,
then he nods.
You hoping she'll let you walk the dog?
I smile.

I hold the tightly wrapped
package of roast beef under my arm
and walk back toward her apartment.
I like the cracks in the old sidewalk,
how they fill with water when it rains.
Inside are tiny ecosystems,
snails and other animals living their own
tiny lives. I wonder if they see me.
I feel like sometimes I live
in my own ecosystem
that nobody else understands.
Maybe, like the snails,
it's okay to just be quiet sometimes.

Mrs. Hershkowitz

ETAN! she calls down,
You're back!
and she lowers a small wicker basket
tied to an old clothesline.
When it reaches me, the basket
has a few coins inside.
I trade the roast beef for the coins,
and she hoists it back up.
I look for her dog in the window,
and as I turn to leave, she calls,
HEY, can you walk Buddy for me, Etan?
I nod, but I am so happy
that I also jump up and down a little.

With some yelping and whining
the dog gets into the basket,
and she slowly lowers him down to me
along with a leash and a small plastic bag.
The dog spins around in the basket,
his bushy tail everywhere,
and at the last moment
lets out a bark and leaps into my arms,
licking my face, his white-and-brown fur
soft on my cheeks, his paws squarely
on my shoulders. *Hey, Buddy*, I say,
Hey, good Buddy, and I hug him back.
Dogs are so easy to talk to.
I set him down, and we head toward the park.

Good Buddy

Buddy loves the park,
a long, green field
at the top of a hill.
He doesn't like to go
into the redwoods. He's a smart dog;
he must know that the grove is a national park
full of animals who already live there.
Instead he runs in giant circles
end to end, pulling me along
until we're tired enough
to lie in the grass.
He licks my face,
then sits with his whole body
over my legs.

Shake-up

I need to get back to the shop
and get Buddy back home.
Walking near the playground
I see Jordan and Martin and two other boys
throwing a baseball around.
I try to ignore them, but it's too late.
Jordan is always with Martin now.
Etan! Wanna play ball with us?
I walk faster.
He won't answer. He doesn't talk anymore.

They laugh at something else, or at me,
but just before I reach the sidewalk
Buddy starts to spin around,
barking and whining.
Martin looks over.
What's wrong with your dog?
I'm trying to calm him down,
and that's when it happens.
The air gets still, the birds go quiet,
the tops of the trees begin to sway
even though there's no wind.
Then the ground shakes
like some giant just stomped down.
We hear car horns, and parents
calling to their kids.
I hold on to Buddy.
Then it ends.

Just a tremor, Martin says.
Probably like, I don't know, 2.4 on the scale.
I start to cross the street,
my legs a little wobbly,
and then, near my right foot,
I see a crack in the pavement,
then I see they are everywhere,
like spiderwebs
crisscrossing the sidewalk.

I bring Buddy back
and stand beneath the window.
Mrs. Hershkowitz is looking out already.
ETAN! Are you okay?
I smile, and she lowers the basket,
speaking in Yiddish the whole time.
I can't understand a word,
but I accept that she may be
saying something like a prayer or a complaint.
Buddy doesn't want to get in the basket;
he licks my face and whimpers into my hands.
Next time, I whisper. *I'll see you soon.*

Just Another Earthquake

I run fast to get back to my grandfather.
Sirens blare, and lots of people are on the street.
When there's an earthquake, we're supposed
to stand in a doorway, wait for the shaking to stop.
Then we go outside and stand in the open,
see if others need help.
It seems like everyone's okay,
it was short, and people are used
to earthquakes around here.
Most of Main Street seems fine, too.
When I get to the shop,
my grandfather is helping Mrs. Li
because one of her tables
toppled over, and the fruit
rolls like marbles in the street.

We get everything arranged,
apples with apples,
persimmons and squash,
and even a few pumpkins
like fat guardians at the edge of her table.
Mrs. Li laughs, and she hugs my grandfather.
It seems like they make each other happy.
He's always there when she needs something.
She makes him soup every single day.
They've been friends since they got here.
Even on the ship,
when things weren't so nice
and they didn't know if
they would even be allowed to stay,
Mrs. Li and my grandmother
tended the kids who were sick
and made sure that everyone had enough food.

It helps, he says, *to go through life together,*
especially since my grandmother is gone.

Mrs. Li asks me if I will do a fast delivery for her.
I look at my grandfather and he nods.
She fills a paper sack with leafy greens,
and then, in another, she puts giant
purple yams! They're heavy,
so I put the bags inside my backpack.
Go to 1401 Forest Road, she says.
If nobody's home, leave it on the steps.
They work in the city, and sometimes they don't answer.

Forest Road is far. Past the park.
So I go as fast as I can.

The Delivery

Ship's Haven is small-town;
we only have a few tall buildings,
three stories high,
not like in the city.
I follow the winding sidewalks,
look at every crack,
wonder if they came
from the earthquake.

Pretty soon the sidewalks end,
and turn into dirt roads
that wind past the redwood park
and into a forest.
The houses are big and old,
with long winding driveways.
My grandfather says that
some of these fancy houses were built
when people got rich in the gold rush.
They were here long before
my grandfather and Mrs. Li
and most of the others on Main Street got here.
But some are just people who work in the city
and need a place to get away.
I walk along the tree-lined paths,
oak, spruce, and fir,
the houses decorated for Halloween
with jack-o'-lanterns in the windows.

1401

I take off my backpack
because I feel like I might break in half.
I didn't know yams could be so heavy.

The house is hidden by trees
down a long driveway,
with a mailbox built like a castle,
a stone tower with a flag on top.
A dragon has its tail wrapped all around it.
I look up and down;
nobody's on the road,
so I lower the red mail flag
and it becomes the dragon's tongue.
It's the greatest mailbox
I've ever seen.

The Door Opens

The house is big and white,
and tangled in vines.
The front door is green,
with a pineapple doorknob,
and outside the door
are rows of shoes in all different sizes.
I am about to place the yams on the doorstep,
when I hear someone singing
Madonna's "Like a Prayer,"
but there's no music, just a voice
from somewhere deep inside.

I take out the paper bags,
balance them in my arms,
and knock.
wait.   wait.   wait.
I knock one more time.
Then, just when I think
I might be able to walk away,
a creak, the knob turns, and the door opens slowly.

It doesn't open far,
only a crack
about the size of my hand.
It's dark inside.
I wait for someone to say hello,
but no one does.
I smell something,
like the oil in the frying pan
when my mother made latkes for Hanukkah.

I wait with the greens and purple yams.
I'm not sure why, but my heart is pounding.
I hear a girl's voice from inside:
>   *You can just leave it.*
Usually, after a delivery, I get a tip,
sometimes a dollar, sometimes candy,
so I wait for a second.
Anything else? she says
through the crack in the door. Silence.
Okay, I think.
I close my backpack and turn
to look at the mailbox one more time.
But then I hear her say something else:
>   *Thanks for bringing the ube.*
I turn around.
They're called ube. Purple yams?
The door starts to shut,
and I glimpse eyes through
the doorway.
See you later, she says.

Remembrance

My grandfather is standing over the old box.
There are books laid out
on his worktable,
and smaller boxes
also made of wood,
folded fabric, an old knife,
some tools,
small sculpted figures,
and a square music box
with a tiny gold crank.
When he looks up at me,
he has tears in his eyes.
Etan. He smiles.
It's been almost fifty years
since we came to Angel Island in 1940.
Fifty years, can you believe it?
He holds up a faded photograph
in black and white.
It's him and a woman
standing on a huge bridge,
with buildings like castles
rising up behind it.
I walk to the table
and pick up the old knife,
turn it around in my hands.
It's my father and mother in Prague.
He looks just like his father, I think.

He picks things up
and puts them down,
each item a key
unlocking something,
but he doesn't enter,
he stays with me
even though I can see in his eyes
he's in a far-off place,
the stories he always tells
coming alive in a new way.

The Knife

I hold up the knife.
Etan, can you get me some tea?
I go and fill the small kettle
in the back, get the mug ready.

You remember what I told you
about Prague,
about leaving to come here?
I do, I remember.
Well, he continues.
Prague was our home.
Our family had lived there
for a very long time,
fighting for our country,
but this time, when the Nazis came . . .
He pauses and takes deep breaths.
I pour water and drop in
a bag of black tea
along with two sugar cubes.
I know this part of the story,
about my great-grandfather,
the great rabbi, and how he had to escape.
I bring my grandpa the tea.
When they came,
we didn't have much time.
Friends helped us.

People looked out for us,
and when it was time
for us to escape,
your great-grandfather stayed behind
so that your grandmother and I
could make our way to Greece
and find the Calypso.

I hold the knife up,
pull it out from its sheath.
Ah, he says, *I almost forgot.*
The knife. My father gave it to me
in case anything happened on the way.
He stays silent, looks at the knife,
then back at me. Then he reaches over
and puts it back into its sheath.

This was everything we had, he says.
We lost two other boxes,
but this one was the most important.
He pats the top of the box
and looks at the spread of objects.
Then he points to one
of two jars in the center of the table.

This one has clay from the Holy Land
and the Vltava River inside it!
He pulls out an old dusty book,
big like the giant Tanakh at our synagogue
or the old Webster's dictionary at school.
On the cover are words in Hebrew
and some other language I've never seen.
There's a picture etched into the leather cover
of a mountain or a hill with eyes and arms
holding the sun in its stumpy hands.

The Golem

That's the golem, Etan.
And some of that,
just the tiniest bit,
is in here.

I remember the stories
about the golem
from Hebrew school,
but I never thought it might be real.

This is the last of the clay
taken from the Vltava River
by your ancestor,
the Maharal himself.

I want to ask him what the Maharal is,
but I can't find the words.
He holds the jar out to me.

It's much heavier than I thought,
and my hands almost fail beneath its weight.

It's the clay of the golem;
it once made a terrible monster
that defended the Jewish people
in their time of greatest need.
I look up, centering the jar in my hands.

It's all our family has left.
The rest is hidden
somewhere far across the sea.

It's almost too much.
I've always believed my grandfather's stories,
but ancient magic?

My grandfather laughs. There's not much left.
Your father, he . . .
Well. That's a story for a different time.

The spirit of the golem
is somewhere else,
but this clay comes
from ancient earth
and ancient waters.
From a world
that no longer fits
with this one.

I look at the other jar;
he lifts it up, staring at it
for a long time.
This is a different kind of clay
from the Dead Sea.

But before he can say more,
my father comes through the door,
blue flannel shirt tied around his waist,
his car keys in one hand,
his face covered in grime.
You ready? he says. *What's all this?*
I watch his eyes move from photo to jar to trinket
and his eyes get bigger.

He's seen this before.
I hold up the knife,
but my father grabs it.
No way, Pop.
Maybe when he's thirteen.
There's silence, and then
a breath.
All right, then. My grandfather smiles.

See you tomorrow, Etan.

Giants

We hurry home because the game
is at Candlestick Park tonight,
Giants against Cubs.
We order pizza and turn up the TV.
I get the notebook,
my father gets his mitt
and hands me mine.
I didn't play in Little League this year.
Next year, right? my father says.
Man, he says, *the Giants
might really do it this year.
Check this out, if they make the Series,
my boss is taking us all to a game.*
He smiles and shoves pizza into his mouth.
Did you feel the earthquake? He looks at me.
I'm working on a roof over in Pacifica, he says.
I felt the building sway a little.
When he says this, my stomach hurts.
I look down at the notebook,
find a green button
stuffed into the pocket.
I think of my mom's scratchy green sweater
and suddenly I feel like
I need to get her the button as fast I can,
but I just hold it up,
try to see through the tiny holes.
I feel his big hand on my shoulder.
*It was fine, just a little shake.
Nothing to worry about.*
I breathe a little, and we watch the game.

Breakfast

I get Cheerios out
and pour them into bowls,
make coffee for Dad
and hot chocolate for me.
He takes a mouthful of cereal.
I have to work late again, okay?
He leans closer.
Try to talk today at school.
To your friends, to anyone.

I don't answer, and I
drink milk from the bowl.

School Days

Mr. Potts is a good teacher.
He talks to me, but he doesn't
try to make me talk back.
When you're ready,
he always says.
      Today I watch the clock.
While I finish my math worksheets and spelling work
I think about ube,
and dragons, and about Buddy,
and the girl behind the door
singing "Like a Prayer"
somewhere in that big house.

Contagious

At lunch everyone goes
to the field to play baseball,
and as usual, they ask me,
but I just want to sit and draw.
I sketch the red flag dragon tongue
on the mailbox, finish shading the stone.
Hey, Jordan says, walking by
and pointing at my picture.
I know that mailbox.
That's the creature's house!

When I hear him say it,
I feel my stomach squeeze;
I think about her eyes in the doorway
and I wonder what he means.
You see her yet? Martin asks.
She's like some kind of creature,
she's got bumps all over her body.
Jordan looks over. *More like scales.*
Don't you remember? I think second grade?
When all of that happened.
But I don't remember.
I heard she gets homeschooled
because she might be contagious and she never leaves the house.

Jordan looks at me and shrugs
almost like he's sorry.

The Library

I think about how terrible it must
feel to be called "the creature."
A creature, I think,
is the golem.
So for the rest of lunch
I go to the library.

If there really is magic clay
in that jar, maybe
I could scrape enough out
to bring a golem to life.
Then it could
        go to the hospital
                and rescue my mom.
I try to imagine
the golem, its strong, gloopy arms
ripping off the hospital doors,
scooping her up,
and carrying her home.
Would it have a human face?

The fountain near the library door
spits water out of a lion's mouth.
        "The Lion of Wisdom,"
                Mrs. McClellan calls it.

The library's one big room,
        shelves stacked
                ceiling to floor;
the smell of old books
                fills the air all around.

Mrs. McClellan is at her big round desk.
She smiles at me.
Behind her are black-and-white photos
of gold rush camps, old San Francisco,
the Angel Island Immigration Station before it burned down,
with a plaque beneath it,
ELLIS ISLAND OF THE WEST.
Under the photos are books on all the places.
When I brought one home once
to show my grandfather,
he didn't want to see it—
didn't want to talk about it.
No one from the *Calypso* likes to talk about Angel Island.

I point to the stack of *World Book Encyclopedias.*
Yes? She runs her finger along the bindings,
        stops at *G* when I nod,
hands me the book. At the table,
I pull out the notebook from my bag,
a pencil, a squishy pink eraser,
then I flip through the pages.
Goalie, gold, golem.

Slowly I take in the pictures.
Dark, lidless eyes set deep into a long skull,
bald, long-necked with painted clay feet.
In one picture, the golem is rising
through a manhole in a city street,
its mouth wide open in the yellow light.

I turn the page, and the next is better, like a short man
made of clay, large eyes and legs,
holding a scroll in its thick arms.

I try to sketch it in my book,
but it looks silly every time,
        like a snowman,
                or a weird gorilla.

I go back to Mrs. McClellan
and check out the book.
She sees my notebook,
raises her eyebrows.
Anything else today?
I smile and shake my head.
Say hello to your grandfather.

Pennants

After school I go right to the shop.
Main Street is busy already.
Everyone has baseball pennants
in their windows or hanging on doors.
Mr. Katsaros's hardware store is green with A's posters,
pictures of all the players and Stomper the elephant.
But in Mr. Osaka's stationery store,
everything is Giants.
I give him a thumbs-up, and he smiles at me.
I like the way the colors look
in the street, like someone painted
it new again,
everyone separate,
        everyone together.

Mrs. Li grabs me.
Etan, I need you to take this
medicine to 1401 Forest Road. Okay?
She hands me a plastic bag with a long tube
inside that looks like it might be toothpaste,
then she fills a paper bag with tea leaves
and folds it all together.

Can you give this to Mrs. Agbayani?
She hands me an apple and two dollar bills.

Before I take the delivery,
I check in with my grandfather to let him know.
He's got some customers inside,
so I wave and hold up the packages,
and he nods.

The Creature

This time I know exactly where to go.
The air is October cool,
with some fog rolling in.
I stop before the house
and try to finish my sketch, to get it just right.
No cars again, just the wide windows
looking over the tall trees.
Then I remember what Martin said,
how she never leaves the house,
and I stop for a moment,
try to look inside the shuttered windows.
All this talk about monsters
and creatures, and now the fog
is coming in thick . . .
it makes me a little scared.
I don't even want to go to the door.
But then, through the windows
from somewhere inside,
I can hear her voice, high and clear;
she sings "Crazy for You."
I stop and listen
but the fog is creepy,
so I ring the doorbell.
She comes right away,
cracks the door open
but stays behind it.
You again? she says.
I want to tell her I like her singing,
but it only comes out as *Your song is . . . um . . .*
What? she cries. *You heard me?*
I nod my head slowly.
It's quiet, but then she laughs,
and it's like the air gets warmer
and the fog lifts just a bit.

I see her eyes
through the doorway
bright and brown
in the foggy afternoon.
So are you just here
to spy on me singing?
Oh, I say, and I pull out the bags.
You don't talk much do you? she says.
What's your name?
Mine? Of course mine, I think, who else—
Etan, I say.
Etan, she repeats.
I like the way she says my name
like the *tan* matters.
For everyone else
the *E* is the main thing.
I'm Malia, she says.
Do you really think
my singing is good?
I nod, and I realize that I'm still holding
the packages. I hand them over to her,
        and that's when I see it.
Her hand looks like a glove,
her wrist and arm
like someone scratched her,
layered scales of skin stacking
one on top of the other.
If I could have stopped time,
I would have kept
my hand from jerking back
when her fingers touched mine.
But she pulls the package in fast.
Thanks, goodbye, she says,
and closes the door.

For Malia

Sorry, I say to the door.
No response.
When I turn toward the road,
I see the fog is thickening.
Then I have an idea.
I take out the notebook
and carefully remove
the picture of the mailbox.
At the very top, I write, "For Malia."
I stand the paper up between two shoes
that I think might be hers,
then I slip away.

I get to the road,
and hear the door open slowly.
Did you draw this?
I turn around and nod.
*It's good! My mom and dad built
that mailbox for me
when I was little.
They say I'm like a princess in a castle.*
I walk back toward the door,
and she's still behind it.
What else do you have in that little book?

She peeks her head out just a bit more,
and I can see her long black hair.
The skin around her eyes is scaly, too.

Do you want to sit down? She points to the porch.
I nod, and then
she sits on the floor,
still behind the door,
a barrier between us,
her body hidden
in the dark house.
I show her the notebook through the crack in the door,
the doodles inside
spinning on the pages.
Sketches of trees
and buildings in San Francisco,
a map of where
my mom's hospital is,
baseball stats,
drawings of every
character in *Star Wars.*
I point to a big drawing
of Chewbacca and smile.
Oh, I love Chewie.
She lets out a *Rawwwr,*
and we laugh.
I feel my voice
in my throat,
the hum of the words
as they come together.
Silence made me forget
what I sounded like.

Voice

She hums into the afternoon air. I like Malia's voice.
Her words feel bright and clear in the air,
and she can make her voice high like a chipmunk
and low like Darth Vader.

Tic-tac-toe

After a little while, two full pages in the notebook
are filled with tic-tac-toe games
that neither of us has won.
I lean my head against the doorway
so I can see a little more,
but the more I lean,
the more she retreats to her side.
I know I should get going.
The road is filled with fog.
I remember my flashlight
in my backpack for the walk home.
I look over to the road.

Fine, she says. *But you BETTER
come back tomorrow.* I nod.
I wonder if Mrs. Li will need me
for another delivery?
I feel the words wanting to jump from my mouth.
I want to ask her if I can bring her something,
but I can't find the words, so I just smile.
She gets up, and so do I.
And almost like
she's read my mind,
she says,

Goodbye, Etan the artist.
Please bring me a pumpkin
if you can.
And for a moment
I see half of her face smiling,
as she closes the door.

Part
2

Shyness

Shyness
is the swirly
part of a glass marble,
all those colors,
a tiny universe
trapped inside
the smallest space.
I've never tried to crack
a marble, but if I did,
I bet the inside
would explode into stars.

Getting Back

It's dark when I finally get back to the shop.
I can see my father through the front window.
He's leaning against the worktable,
smiling with my grandfather;
the steam from their cups
rises between them.
They look happy.
It's been harder
since my mom's gone away.
My grandfather wants
us to spend more time at synagogue,
but my father won't.
I almost don't want to interrupt them.
I wonder if he had to wait long?
What if he's mad?

Well, says my grandfather,
looks who's returned.

My father stiffens for a moment,
but when I walk to the table,
my grandfather puts his arms around me,
his heavy hands around my shoulders.
If you keep doing all these deliveries,
you better start taking your bike.
I feel his body relax, and mine does, too.

I get my backpack,
see the dark greenish box
on the low shelf in the back room,
and notice something strange.
         There is a smell:

    wet dirt,
            pond water,
                 the ground
                          after a hard rain.
         I want to look inside the heavy lid.

My grandfather
walks me toward the door
where my father is already standing.

Etan, he coughs through his words,
Jordan's mother came by today
to pick up a necklace
I fixed for her.
She said you should call him,
invite him to Shabbos? All right?
I see my father's eyes
go from me to my grandfather
and back again.
Then he puts his hands
on my shoulder.
See you tomorrow, Pop.

Jordan

Jordan can steal bases
better than any other kid in our school.
My father used to leave work early
to take us to the park,
teach us how to steal bases,
catch a fly ball without flinching,
how to hit grounders.
You can try different stances,
but the neutral stance is my favorite.
He looked out across the field.
No one can guess where you might hit.
But you can try different ones
until you find what's comfortable.
I don't love playing baseball,
but with Jordan it was always fun.
He's so fast, if he can get on base,
he can steal the next one.

It's all in the hips
that's where the power is.
Jordan learned it right away,
his stable front foot,
the slight lift, the swing;
it's like the baseball
just gets huge in his eyes.

One day, when I struck out
three times in a row,
found myself crying
in the dugout,
Jordan was there,
telling me:
     Don't quit. Try again.
                    Like a real friend should.

The best part was always after.
We went to Farrel's for triple scoops
and talked about Rickey Henderson
stealing bases like no one else.

Spring afternoons,
baseball and ice cream,
the sun cutting through the fog
          was enough for my father
                    to leave work early.

I think in some ways
it was harder for my dad
when Jordan's parents
decided we should stop
spending time together
because they thought my
mom wasn't safe anymore.

Our dads yelled at each other,
and we didn't really know
what to do, so we just
                    stopped talking.

Asking the Question

My father turns the Giants game on the car radio.
The announcer is talking about
the Giants' chances of beating the Cubs,
winning the National League,
Making it all the way.

My father looks at me.
So, how was your day?
You sure were late.
I feel all the words about Malia
rush from my stomach
to my throat,
but instead I push them down
because I also think about
my mom, and Jordan,
and it's too hard,
so I say nothing.

Can you at least talk to me about it?
He raises his voice a little, his hands thump
against the steering wheel slightly.
I can tell he's frustrated.

My father turns onto our little street.
The fog is lighter now,
and the moon is slicing
                        through the sky.

Look, Etan, I know it's hard.
It's hard for me, too.
Your grandpa thinks
we should talk to the rabbi.
There's no way I'm going to,
but maybe ... maybe you should?

I quietly breathe deep breaths,
imagine Jordan's room
filled with Rickey Henderson posters
and baseball trophies,
     comics spread out
          across his floor.
Maybe I could just call him,
but today everything feels like too much.

My mom tells me
that some days are like that.
I am all out of words,
so instead I reach for my father's hand
and he puts it around me,
                    and we watch the moon
shining through the fog.

Try to Speak

I miss school in the morning
because I need to go to my appointment.
Sometimes on Fridays
I see a doctor about how
to deal with my mom being gone.

The doctor asks me
if I've been trying to speak at school.
I am able to tell him: *Sometimes*.
He says, try raising your hand once per day,
        answer a question,
        say hello to a teacher,
        play with your friends.
        Take a step of some kind.

When we first came to see him
I thought he might have answers
to why my words disappeared,
but all he talks about
is finding them
again.

Where Did My Words Go?

I draw a blue river,
willow trees
bent over
        rushing water
                flowing down
around giant boulders,
where some of the words
                        float:
baseball, Jordan,
        mother, Malia,
words that find their way
to a waterfall flowing
into the sea.
Words that
        drop, one by one,
                into the salt and blue.

Talent Show

After school, where I did not raise my hand
and managed to avoid
baseball at recess,
I run to Main Street because
even though it's Shabbat,
there might be another delivery.

When I reach our street,
I look up to the third-story window
but Buddy isn't there,
the window is shut.
Two blocks down,
near Grace Covenant Community Center,
I see four ladies in bright feathered hats.
My grandfather calls them
the Covenanteers.
We like them because
they bring cupcakes to school,
run the book fairs, help with our after-school program,
but they also love to have long conversations with kids,
so I try to avoid them.
     Etan, one of them calls.
She hands me a red paper.
     Etan, please come to our youth group's
     Harvest Festival Talent Show!
I don't say anything,
so she just smiles,
hands me the flyer.
     Yes, well, singing, dancing, you name it.
     It's going to be wonderful!

On the paper
is a picture of a giant
jack-o'-lantern,
musical notes,
and the words

HARVEST FESTIVAL
TALENT SHOW
AND SPAGHETTI SUPPER
GRACE COVENANT YOUTH GROUP
TUESDAY, OCTOBER 17TH
4:00
SINGERS, DANCERS, ACTORS,
ALL ARE WELCOME

I take the paper,
fold and fit it into my pocket,
then take off down the street as fast I can.

Paper Bag

My grandfather is cleaning up his shop,
fitting screws and nails into the right containers,
a long row of old jars and soup cans,
each with a different size screw
for every watch or necklace ever made.
I drop my bag near the workbench.
He's coughing, but he reaches out his hand and smiles.
He spills the screws into my hand.
I'm good at finding the tiny slots for the smallest screws.
Make sure all the lids are closed tight,
we don't want these falling everywhere.
I start to press the lids down on the long row,
but then the door opens.

Mrs. Li walks in.
        Good afternoon, gentlemen.
A paper bag the size of a football in her hands.
Smiling, she walks straight up to me,
opens the bag, pulls out a huge, red fruit,
and holds it up in front of my eyes.
        Do you know what this is?
I look at my grandfather,
who is polishing a metal cup.
I shake my head.

She hands it to me.
It's as big as my hand,
and the outside is hard like a beetle shell,
or a baseball.
        Inside, she says, *are deep red seeds that pop into the*
        sweetest juice.
        It's a pomegranate. It can soothe the skin on the inside.
        Can you bring it to the Agbayanis?

She looks at my grandfather.
Tomorrow morning he can.
He smiles. *Will you be joining us,*
Mrs. Li? For Shabbos?
She puts the pomegranate
back into the bag and rolls it tightly.
Not tonight, she says,
and walks out of the store.

A Different Shabbat

It used to be different.
All of us together around the table,
my grandparents, Mrs. Li, Mr. Cohen,
Jordan's family, people from temple
and the shops on Main Street,
my parent's friends.

I helped my mom bake challah,
and on warm days we would
set it out to rise in the sun.

The past few months
have been just the three of us,
and sometimes Mrs. Hershkowitz and Buddy.
We usually have pizza now,
and sometimes my grandfather
will bring challah from the bakery
if he can get there on time.
Tonight, he gets the best kind,
     long loaves with
          toasted poppy seeds.

We light the candles,
and he blesses us,
     puts some dollar bills
          into the tzedakah box,
          saving money for those in need.
We sing out the prayers,
and I see my father moving his lips
but no sound coming out.

It's been a long time since I've heard his voice
say any kind of prayer,
and here, without a thought,
my body and mind remember
the words to bless and welcome in the Sabbath.
I say them out loud, my regular voice, alive.
They look at me, and my stomach rumbles,
and then I tear the biggest
piece of challah I can, dip it into a pool of honey,
and shove it into my mouth.
My father lifts the challah,
breaks it in half like he's the Incredible Hulk,
and throws the other half to my grandfather,
and we see who can shove the most challah
into their mouth at once.

After Shabbat

We sit back in our chairs,
while the wax slowly melts
as the candles burn down.
In the notebook, I add words in black lettering
against the blue water of my river drawing.
Shabbat,
    candles,
challah,
    family.
My father and grandfather talk about the Giants.
The sounds of their voices flow like the water
in my drawing around marsh reeds and giant boulders.

It's when I press the tip of the pencil
to the edge of the letter *b*
to write *baseball*
that the table
    suddenly
        jerks
back and forth,
snaps the tip of my pencil,
and then we hear the shaking
of the dishes in the cabinets,
like they might all break at once.
Then for a moment it's still,
and we breathe, but the ground
is still moving in a low rumble.
First, far away, and then closer
and closer like ocean waves
crashing beneath the earth.
All of our earthquake drills have taught us what to do,
so I get under the table as quick as I can.
The overhead light swings.

My father gets under with me,
and we see the candles in their silver holders
tilting back and forth.
My grandfather reaches them just before they fall,
then climbs underneath the table, too.
By the time he gets there, everything is still,
and we hear the sounds of people outside,
loud voices calling out for each other.
  Wait.
My grandfather
holds both of our hands.
  Close your eyes.

I put a hand on the floor
as if I might feel the earth move.

He says a prayer,
and my father looks straight at him.
The two candles roll beneath the table,
turn us amber in their dull glow.
My father quickly snuffs them out.

The Alarm

My father puts on his tool belt
and starts to inspect the apartment.
Then we go into the hall to see if we can help.
The doors to other apartments are wide open.
Neighbors wander in the hallway,
TVs and radios blare. Then, at the far end
I see a brown-and-white streak
bounding down the stairs.
Buddy runs through the legs of the people
in the hall and jumps right up onto me,
licks my face.
Hey, boy, are you okay?
I feel his soft fur.
He whines a little,
then he jumps down,
turns and pads down the hall and looks back at me,
tail wagging.
My grandfather comes behind me,
whispers, *Let's not wait when our four-legged friend
comes to tell us something*.

I don't know if Buddy meant it
or if we would have checked anyway,
but when we get upstairs
we find Mrs. Hershkowitz
sitting in the dark.
Ruth! My grandfather runs in.
  *The lights are broken,
  and here I am on the floor
  with no way to stand*, she says.
My grandfather shuffles into the kitchen.
It must be a breaker, he says.

He flips switches until the lights come on.
She looks like a little girl sitting there,
in her gray braids and her nightgown,
stacks of books all over the floor.
She was a librarian in the city for so many years,
and books are everywhere,
usually piled high into towers,
but now most of the books
have toppled onto the floor.
We help her up to the table,
put her walker near her.

We pick up the books, stack them on the ground.
My grandfather gets her a glass of water,
and I make sure Buddy has food.
We check around the apartment
to make sure nothing else is broken.
My grandfather tests her China cabinet.
We should nail this down, Ruth.
I'll come do it soon.

She makes us eat cookies.
> *You know my aunt lived through the*
> *San Francisco earthquake in 1906.*
> *It wasn't the shaking, she said.*
> *It was the fire. It burned four days and four nights.*
> *Everything burning because of ham and eggs.*

We look at each other.
I expect my grandfather to know everything.
Sometimes I forget that he came here in 1940.
> *Some woman on Hayes Street,*
> *cooking ham and eggs for breakfast,*
> *the gas stove, it started everything.*

She laughs. *You think I'm silly?*
  It's the everyday things
  we need to be careful of.
  We think we know so much,
  that science and TV have all the answers.
Her voice grows louder.
  But we should learn from what happens to us!
She looks straight at me.
I want to say something, but I don't have any words.
She puts her hand softly on my head.
  Thank you.

Bareket

Before my father takes him home,
my grandfather sits on my bed
to tell me good night.
Exciting Shabbos, wouldn't you say?
I nod, my body feels awake,
but my mind is tired.
Etan, I have not heard your voice enough today.
Can you tell me good night?
Usually I don't have too much trouble
speaking to him,
but when someone asks me to speak,
everything around me grows bigger and bigger
and I become small.

He pulls a small bag from his coat pocket,
a leather pouch tied tightly.
He coughs quietly, unties the pouch,
and empties it into his hand.
I sit up. He is holding a green stone.
It shines, even in the dim light.
This, he says, *is a bareket,*
an emerald, an ancient, powerful stone,
like from the breastplate of Aaron!
Feel it. He centers it in my hand.
It's the size of a quarter, feels smooth,
even soft, but when I hold it to the light,
I can almost see through it. I look up.
        Did this come from? I think.
The box? He can read my mind. *Yes. An ancient treasure.*
There are many things in the box,
but for you I thought of this one.

Your heart has been a little closed up.
This might help open it up again.
When you feel afraid to speak,
hold the stone in your hand,
tight tight tight,
and it will bring you courage.

He closes my fingers
around the smooth stone,
bends down toward me,
and brings his lips just close enough
to whisper the words
   Good night.

The Delivery

The brown paper bag
rests carefully in the fruit bowl,
the pomegranate treasure buried inside.
    Good morning, sunshine.
My father's on the couch drinking coffee,
watching highlights of the Giant's game.
I pour myself some cereal and sit next to him.

Hey, so I am caulking roof tiles
at my job in Pacifica,
I could at least drop you off for your delivery?
I jump up,
change my clothes, get my backpack,
stuff it full of granola bars,
an apple, and a handful of licorice.
I pull out the notebook
to make sure my drawing of the river is inside.
I open it, and a red flyer sails out of the pages.
What's this? My father picks it up.
Youth group talent show?
Did the Covenanteers get ya?
I nod. He looks at me.
Are you thinking of . . .
But before he can finish, his eyes go wide.
Oh, I see, the seventeenth.
Remember that if I get tickets
for the series—WHEN I get tickets—
there might be a game that night.
I stick the flyer in my notebook,
and we head out the door,
the bag of pomegranates heavy in my hands.

The Phone Rings

Close the door behind you, Etan.
My father's already down the hall.
His truck keys dangle in his hand,
and the phone rings.
        Ring . . .
I stare.
        Ring . . .
ETAN! my father calls from the stairwell.
        Ring . . .
I find the green stone in my pocket and squeeze.

Then all at once
my feet shake loose,
and I walk to the phone,
pick it up, and say . . . *Hello?*
Etan! Her voice
sends relief into my body,
and words fight in my stomach and my throat
to be the first ones out.
Hi, Mom! I say.
Are you okay? she asks.
        It was quite a shake.
Then, like a faucet
turned on, sputtering at first,
then fully opened,
my words pour out
and I tell her about
the earthquake, and Buddy,
and how I'm doing deliveries,
about carrying her notebook everywhere,
and Malia, and Grandfather's shop.
I look up and see my father, smiling in the doorway.
He nods and waits outside.

We talk for a long time
and never once does she ask me if I'm talking at school.
I tell her, *I'm about to deliver some pomegranates.*
She pauses. *Well, you'd better go, then.*

She tells me she'll see me soon.
                    Sooner than I think.

Forest Road

My father drives the back way
to Forest Road, where it climbs into the foothills.

Some of the tallest redwoods are here,
an ancient grove, my grandfather says,
and the houses are far apart.

My father drives slowly.
Would be nice to live up here. He stops
at one house with a redbrick driveway,
and massive white columns
that reach to huge windows.
> *Look, see that little cabin in the back?*
> Behind the garage, I see an old
shack, like in a movie,
made of logs and twisted branches.
> *That's an original log cabin from the gold rush.*
> *Those things were all over this place*
> *when the gold rush started.*
> *Different now, isn't it?*

It is, I whisper.

He looks at me like every word I say
might mean I'm all better.

Have you met the family yet?
I shake my head no.
Yeah, they are busy people.

I see 1401 in the distance,
the castle mailbox and the dragon
spinning around it.

We stop at the driveway.
        You going to be all right, Etan?
        Go straight to the shop after, okay?
        I'll get you there later.
I smile, watch him turn the truck around,
wave.

The house looks the same,
the mailbox, the shoes by the door,
only this time, the driveway is full of cars.

Pomegranates

I hold the bag of pomegranates from the bottom.
The paper is about to rip.

Every time I've made a delivery
it's been during the week,
so her parents must have been at work.
Today I notice shoes I haven't seen at the door,
and sandals, and a walking stick
leaning against a bench.

The pineapple doorknob turns as I walk up
and then the door
     opens
          wide.
A woman with long black hair
smiles at me, steam rising
from the cup in her hand.

I have to find a word to say.
Be polite. Make eye contact.
I want to reach for the green stone
in my pocket,
but I'm afraid the bag might break,
so I just hold it up in front of my face.

Good morning, what's this? she says.
Her voice is kind.

Inside I see the living room
and the kitchen are connected into one giant room
with puffy couches, a TV, paintings over a fireplace,
and a wide stairway at the very end.

In the kitchen,
there's an older woman reading at the counter,
but I don't see Malia.

What's your name?
But before I can try to answer,
I hear a voice from behind her.
ETAN! This is my mom!
Malia wraps her arms
around her mom's waist and peeks out.
I can't help but notice the bumps
like tiny scales spread
in broken patterns on her arms,
stopping and starting,
      red,   raw,
in between
      brown patches
of smooth,
      perfect skin.
Mom, this is Etan,
he's bringing all the stuff from Mrs. Li.

Nice to meet you, Etan,
I'm Mrs. Agbayani, Malia's mother.
She's told us about you.
Would you like to come in?

Malia's arms tighten
when her mom says this, and she slides
farther behind her.

I walk through,
        slowly,
Malia staying
carefully behind her mom.

The kitchen smells like cooking oil, garlic, and
other spicy things.

You can put those on the table, Malia's mom says.
Oh, and this is my mother, Malia's Lola.
You can call her Lola, too.
I set the bag down on the counter.
Lola looks at me.
        Kain ka na!
She takes some egg rolls
from the small pot on the stove
and puts them on a paper plate,
plops a spoonful of a red sauce in the center,
and slides it over to me.
That's lumpia, Malia says. *It's the best food*
in the universe. THE UNIVERSE.
There's a sudden silence,
and I notice all eyes on me.
Try it, Etan! I take a bite.
I've had egg rolls before,
but this is different, crispier, saltier,
filled with meat and vegetables.
I take another bite,
and they start to talk again.
Don't mind Lola, Malia says.
She prefers to speak Tagalog.

Lola smiles at me, reaches into the paper bag,
pulls out a pomegranate.
She says something to Mrs. Agbayani,
and then there's a swirl
of words in Tagalog,
but I recognize the quick tone,
the frustrated breaths.
I know it well.
      They are arguing.

I Should Leave

I shouldn't be here. I put my backpack on
and wipe my mouth.
But just then, Malia steps in front of me.
She's wrapped in a thin blanket
with musical notes in different patterns.
She looks like a wizard with the blanket
around her, her face
half covered, one brown eye,
half a nose, half a mouth.
Do you want to come outside with me?

Her mom puts out her hand.
Malia, it's too sunny. Wait for the fog.
Please, Mom, please. See, I'm covered up.
Malia pulls the blanket around
her shoulders. Her black hair
pokes out in all directions.
Mrs. Agbayani smiles.

C'mon! Malia shouts.
She grabs a pomegranate and leads me through the living room,
past the biggest TV I've ever seen, past a room
that has a pool table,
and then down a few stairs and through a door that opens
onto a sudden green lawn
against tall redwoods.

Trees Are Friends

These trees are my friends,
their branches keep my skin out of the sun.
Malia walks across the grass with light steps;
the music-note blanket flutters behind her.
She stands between two large trees,
looks back at me, and then waves for me to follow.

Through the two trees
a path winds down a bank of soft earth, longleaf ferns
and red, polka-dot mushrooms growing along the stones.
Malia walks barefoot, the bottom of the blanket gathering
up pieces of fern and specks of dirt
until it's filthy.

Jordan and I explored forests,
but I've never been here,
too private, too far,
where the trees seem bigger
than any trees I've seen before.
Malia says, *They're old,*
                very old.
                        The oldest trees in the West.
                        I've always been able to feel the trees,
                        even when I was little.
How? I ask. She looks at me
with half her face.
        They tell me.
        They are the oldest trees
        and they have LOTS to say
        about all kinds of things.

Wisdom

I stare at her.
I feel words wanting to flow out of me.
My fist closes around the green stone in my pocket.

What do trees say? I ask.
She puts her hand on a redwood trunk.

I get closer,
and almost in a whisper,
>   *People are young,*
>   *they don't see what they should.*
>   *They only see what they want to see.*

I don't understand.
>   *You **know** what I mean, Etan.*
>   *People should know that it's okay if **you** don't like to talk,*
>   *or go to school,*
>   *or anything.*
>   *That should be okay.*
>   *Trees understand this.*
>   *They can feel you, even when you're quiet.*
>   *They are excellent listeners.*

This makes sense to me.
Once, on a field trip to Golden Gate Park,
we learned about how plants
can sense vibrations.

I put my hand on the trunk of another tree
looking up up up into its high, green branches.
I whisper to it, tap on the trunk,
imagine it feeling my sound.
Listening.

Singing to the Trees

It can hear you,
I promise.
Malia turns down the path
and begins to sing "Time After Time."

If you're lost you can look
and you will find me . . .

I imagine the trees
bending their piney branches
to the sound of her voice.

Then she stops
in a beam of sunlight.

Without thinking,
I look at her, remembering what her mom said,
and she knows what I'm thinking.

My skin. My skin,
it's too thin, they say.
Or my mom says
I might be allergic to sunlight.
My dad says it's just bad eczema.

      I can't help but scrunch my eyes.
      I've never heard of anyone being allergic to sunlight.
They are both doctors,
so they have lots of theories,
but mostly they argue about me.

No one really knows
why my skin does what it does.
Most people have rashes that itch.
I have itches that rash.
It's actually feeling okay right now.
But sometimes, well . . .

and then she's quiet.

The Magic Pool

We walk down a path,
slow and winding.
I hear water, a small stream,
at the bottom
where water spills into a small pool,
before it rushes on.
Large stones rest on the banks.
This is my favorite spot. She looks around.
These are the Sitting Stones.
This is where the trees listen the most.
The pool is magical.
We sit on the rocks and she hums.
She holds the pomegranate up to her nose and breathes deeply.
I try to see the magic in the pool
as bugs skim across its surface
and the sunlight glimmers on the water.
Malia walks to the edge, dips her hand in,
lets the water filter through her fingers.
I'm not even supposed to go in water.
It dries my skin.
But this water is magic.
She stands and twirls so the blanket flies.
One day, I will come here
and wash away all the bad skin.

Sunlight streams
to the bottom of the pool.
It's not very deep, and it's clear.
I put my hand down to the bottom.
It's clay. All clay.
I pull up the wet goop, and Malia steps back, laughing.
It's not THAT magical.
Better not get any on me.

I think about my grandfather
and the old treasure box in his shop
and the jars of magic clay from the Dead Sea
and the Vltava River.
Is all clay the same?
Why is this clay any different?
I let the clay drip from my fingers,
wash off the rest in the cool water.

This stream comes all the way
from the mountains where they once found gold,
and then it flows all the way
into the sea. It's a very old stream.

My Drawing

I take out the notebook, mutter the words
    Can I show you?
YES! Malia shouts.
I pull out the paper
where I drew the river
under the question
"Where do my words go?"

She looks at it for a long time,
circles around me three times,
making noises, *Mm-hmm, uh-huh,*
over-exaggerating each sound,
almost like she's talking to a whole group.
She glances at the trees, then back to the picture.
Well, she says, stepping up on the rock,
gesturing to the trees surrounding us.
It's unanimous.
I look around.

We love it!
It's just right.

Flyer

We sit in the small clearing
near the stream, and she tells me
about how she tried go to school,
but her skin kept getting sick,
and then "the incident" happened,
so now she goes to school at home.
She doesn't really go anywhere
except sometimes to her cousins' houses.
I want to ask her about the incident, but I stay quiet.

It's hard to imagine that life.
I flip through the notebook
and in the breeze a few papers fly out,
and the red flyer floats into the air,
sails back and forth, and settles faceup.
Talent show? Malia says, picking it up.

I stand near her,
point to the word *singing* on the flyer.
    You could sing, I say quietly, smiling.

She pulls the blanket
        tighter around her face.
We stand in silence,
the water from the stream gurgling slowly past.
She looks at me. *I will have to consult with the forest.*
She wraps the blanket, which she calls Blankie,
so that a treble clef rests where her mouth should be
and walks off into the towering trees.

Ripples in the Water

Wind through branches
    and fern leaves,
        quiet water over smooth stones.
Malia's voice softly singing to the trees.
I hold the green bareket.
If my grandfather found *this* for me,
I wonder if he could help Malia, too?
Maybe there is a stone that can help her skin?

Then her voice stops,
a sudden quiet,
like someone turned everything off.

I see small ripples in the pool,
like an invisible stone
dropped in its center.
And then, all at once,
the trees begin to sway
back and forth,
except there is
    no wind at all.
Then, a rumble in the ground,
a sudden jerk,
the foot of a giant
stepping down.
    I look for Malia.
The trees shake faster,
the tops of their trunks bend and sway;
in the distance, I hear a loud crack
like everything
    breaking
        all at once.
Then
    suddenly
        it stops.

Silence.

      The birds begin again.
I stand there, frozen,
trying to find the courage to look for her,
feeling the unstoppable words rise into my mouth.
I shout her name and start toward the woods.
My arm catches on a sharp branch
and I feel the bark scrape my skin.
When I look down, drops of blood are already forming.
I cover it with my shirt sleeve
because suddenly I see her running toward me,
but she looks different. The blanket is gone.

The Face

What did I expect to see?
An actual creature, a monster?
Instead, I see her,
long black hair, the deep brown eyes.
On half her face, the side usually covered by her blanket,
the skin is red, bumpy, scaly,
almost ripped open, the skin around
her eye swollen to twice its size,
making her eye hard to see.
I hear Martin's voice in my head,
The creature . . . , but I ignore it.
She throws her arms around me,
buries her face on my shoulder.
I hug her
the way I like to be hugged when I need it.

> *I'll never get used to that*, she says.
> *It's like the only solid thing,*
> *the only safe thing,*
> *the earth itself*
> *is coming apart.*

She jerks back, like she's forgotten something.
No, she cries, *no* . . .
She tries to cover her face and
searches the ground for Blankie.
I follow her to the stream
where Blankie floats
at the edge of the shore.
She picks up the sopping blanket,
and together we squeeze out the water.

Sometimes You Don't Need Words

I try to make Malia feel better.
It's okay, I say.
She scowls, her eyes tighten.
> *I'm just glad you*
> *yelled my name.*
> *Does it take an earthquake*
> *to bring your voice to life?*

We squeeze the blanket one more time,
get our stuff, walk back up
the path toward her house.
On the way, Malia touches the bark
of every tree on the path,
and so do I.

It's Okay

When her mom sees her,
she runs to us, full speed,
wet-faced with tears,
and Malia starts to cry, too.

Her mom puts out a hand for me to come.
I feel her arm on my back
pressing me close.

Malia, what were you thinking!
I told you not to go down there.
Then more hugging, and by now Lola joins us.
Come, she says, and takes
my hand, and we all walk back inside.

Broken Glass

Lola looks at my arm,
the scratch is deep.
You okay?
For some reason when she asks me,
the words pour out.
     Yes, it was kinda scary.
Lola smiles.

Inside, the paintings on the wall are sideways,
and in the kitchen, cabinet doors
are flung open and glass is shattered
on the floor.

We walk in with our shoes on.
Lola cleans off my arm, puts a Band-Aid on it.
Malia's mom hands us brooms and dustpans,
        and we sweep.
I'm good at sweeping. I've helped out Mrs. Li
and everyone else on Main Street.
It feels good to help.

When we are done cleaning,
we each take a glass of mango juice,
and Lola carries a basket of soft rolls
outside to an old picnic table.
Malia's blanket is once again
wrapped around her.

Right as we sit down,
I feel words rising up,
unstoppable like exhaling:
     Thank you.
You are welcome, Etan! Lola says.
Malia stares at me with one eye.
I think she's impressed.

Pandesal

I eat at least five of the fluffy bread rolls,
some with cheese baked inside, some with raisins.
Lola says, *You like the pandesal?*
Yes! I mumble with
bread in my mouth.
We laugh.
          Hey, Etan, show them a mailbox picture!
Oh yes, please,
her mom says, sipping her tea.

I take out the notebook,
open to some sketches of the mailbox,
and they point out the different textures,
the way the dragon curls.
Malia flips through pages of doodles,
and I see one from my mom,
a baseball with flowers growing out of it.
Eventually, Malia gets
to the picture of the river,
and her mom and Lola take their time
to read each word, follow every waterline
along the inky banks.

I look at Malia, and I notice
she's scratching her arm inside her blanket.
I hadn't realized it
because it's been hidden,
but I can see the way her arm moves.
She has been scratching almost the whole time.

Etan. I look up at Mrs. Agbayani.
*This is very poetic, about your words
          and where they go.*
I smile. I don't know how to react.

Her mom flips the page,
and the red flyer unfolds itself.
I reach out and hold it up.

Hmm, a talent show?
I push the flyer toward Mrs. Agbayani.
Oh well. She wraps her arm around Malia.
Malia whispers, *He wants me to sing.*
We'll see, her mom says,
but I know what it means
when a parent says *We'll see.*
It usually means
I don't want to say no right now,
but it is no all the way.

Malia smiles at me,
raises her eyebrow up and down
like she's hatching a plan,
like she has it all
            under   control.

Just before Mrs. Agbayani gives me a ride
back to my grandfather's shop,
Malia walks around the front yard with me,
constantly scratching her arm,
and I can't ignore it.
Is your arm okay?
        What? Oh. Yes.
She looks up at the branches of a tree near the road,
gently touches its bark.
Maybe she's listening to it.

Do you really think I can sing? she asks.
Yes! I say, *you're so good . . .*
She looks back at the tree
and I stare at it, too,
our bellies full of pandesal.
It feels like we both
have run out of words.
Sometimes silence
is just what you need.

A car passes by slowly;
Malia waves. Then she turns to me
with a sideways smile
and punches my arm
just enough to hurt.
      Good singer? she says.
      I'm a great singer.
We look at each other,
      silence,
           then we laugh.
Etan, it's not the singing.
I can't because—I mean—well, this.
And for the second time,
she removes Blankie slightly,
lets me see her full face.
Oh, I say. I want to tell her
that it doesn't matter.
She should be herself,
but I know the truth is not so easy.

Pumpkin

Before I get in the car,
Malia runs up to me.
Oh, Etan, you forgot something.
I look at her,
think of the bag of pomegranates.
My pumpkin?
     I forgot. I whisper. *Next time?*
But the best part
is now
     I have a reason
               to come back.

Grown-up Talk

Mrs. Agbayani talks to me,
but she doesn't ask me any questions,
and that makes me feel safer.
Grown-ups like to ask questions that are impossible to answer.
>*I'm so glad for you, Etan;*
>*Malia is so happy when you come.*

I look at her, and now it's me who wants to ask the questions
about her skin, and her eye, and being allergic to the sun.
But I don't know how to ask,
so I just say, *Is she going to be okay?*
>I feel the car slow down
>as we come into town.

Mrs. Agbayani stares
straight ahead, wiping her eyes.
We are trying everything, she says.
There is a new cream at the hospital
that's supposed to bring some relief.
Her father will bring some home soon.
To me, it sounds like she is talking to herself.

Mrs. Agbayani parks in front of my grandfather's shop.
I see him through the window
in the warm light,
tinkering or something.
He looks up, sees us, his face
unfolds into a smile.
He unlocks the door and comes out fast,
hugs me.
She smiles.
>*We're okay.*
>*Just a scratch on his arm.*
>*He'll be fine.*

More earthquakes
than I can remember
in a long time.

He nods.
      This is a good boy you have here, she says.

I don't know, my grandfather replies,
I think he's hiding something.

She laughs,
but then, something else.
She walks over to my grandfather,
and he hugs her, tight.
Like only he can,
like she's family.
It's been too long, he says.
How's your mother?
They talk for a while,
then she walks across the street
to where Mrs. Li
is closing her storefront.
They hug and then walk
together arm in arm.
Come inside, Etan, my grandfather says.
Have you eaten?

Not Hungry

My grandfather slides me a plate
of pickled herring and a giant slice of pumpernickel,
then he goes back to wiping off an old board
with a special cloth covered in slick oil or something.
The smell of herring mixed with the oil
makes my stomach feel weird.
It's good to see Mrs. Agbayani.
I look at him. I know
they came here on the *Calypso*,
but he never really talks about them.

The Journey

My grandfather tells me:
Malia's mom, Mrs. Agbayani, is the daughter
of Emelita and Enrique Urbano.
Enrique was an inventor—and a good one!
He came a few years earlier,
on a different ship
before all of us.
While he was waiting for Lola,
he was working, inventing.
But in the years of saving money
the laws changed, and it wasn't easy for them to come anymore,
so the only way to make it was on one of the last boats.
The Calypso.
We met Emelita when the Calypso *stopped in the Philippines.*
Enrique had sent for her.
He coughs. *It was such a long journey.*
My grandfather stares at me.
I try to listen the best I can.

Lola

He can see the surprise on my face.
I think about all the people from the *Calypso*
at our family gatherings, even Shabbat dinners,
but I can't remember the Agbayanis being there.
How come we don't see them more? I ask.
He closes the jar of oil,
folds the cloth over the top of it,
takes a deep breath.

> *It was hard for us when we came over,*
> *but it was even harder for them.*
> *Not everyone was treated the same way.*
> *Emelita always kept to herself.*
> *She used to come to our meetings*
> *before you were born.*
> *She even helped watch your father sometimes*
> *when he was small.*
> *I don't think he remembers.*
>
> *They moved out to 1401 Forest Road.*
> *It's a very old house, so they fixed it up over the years.*
> *That's where Emelita had her children*
> *and where her family lives now,*
> *including your Malia!*
>
> *She spent a lot of time in the Philippines*
> *after Enrique died,*
> *but I think she's back here for good.*
> *She wants to be with her family,*
> *and I'm glad.*

A Day of Awe

Tell me about your day, Grandfather says.
Where were you when the earthquake happened?

I take a bite of the brown bread,
push the plate away.
    I was okay. I had this.
I hold up my green bareket,
then try to tell him everything I can,
words here and there,
about the Agbayanis
and the forest and the pool
and about Malia,
and Blankie and pandesal.
I don't stop until the brown bread
is all nibbled away.

My throat feels dry from talking so much,
and I can see my grandfather is surprised because
he's nodding and smiling
with his lips pushed out.

He grabs my face with both of his giant hands.
This is great, Etan, perfect timing for Rosh Hashanah.
We have much to be in awe about.
We look inward, and rejoice outward!
You should tell the rabbi about all of this.

Then I notice something strange.
Something out of place.
The old wooden treasure box
is right next to him
on the floor, the lid slightly open.

Part
3

Clay

My grandfather wipes the board one last time,
sets the cloth down.
Go lock the door. Let me show you something.
He reaches into the box, pulls out the two
small jars the size of softballs,
with Hebrew letters I still can't read.
He lifts the jar that held
the clay for the golem,
looks at it, and sets it aside.

> He says a prayer,
> lights a short candle
> melted into an old plate,
then reaches for the other jar.
> *What is that?* I ask.
Shhhh, he whispers.
> *Watch*.
He slowly unlatches
the old metal lock
but starts coughing and his hands shake.
I walk toward him, but he stops me,
then with all his might, he dips two fingers inside.
He stops coughing, looks at me.
> *Come here*.
The flame of the candle
> is bright, burning brighter,
> > flickering wild
> > > in wind that isn't there.

He reaches out for my arm,
clutches me near the scratch
and a little blood oozes out.
Grandpa, I say, because
his grip is so strong and his face looks different,
younger, like a man from a different time.

Etan, there are many things
from the old world
from your ancestors
that we carry with us always.
It's our fire. Our light.
He squeezes my arm each time
like he's pressing the words into my blood.
But there are some things from those times that are still with us.
He pulls his fingers from the jar.
They are smeared with a dark, pasty clay
impossibly wet, dripping back into the jar.

Changes

He pulls me close,
presses down his two clay fingers
on the cut on my arm.
     It's cold,
         like standing in the snow
         with no shoes.
My whole body shivers.
He slides the clay over my cut,
pushes it into the shallow wound,
and with his other hand
he presses on my heart,
singing something low in Hebrew.
     The candle goes out
              in a wisp of smoke.
The shop is dark and silent.
Etan? I feel warmth return to my body.
He loosens his grip and carefully scrapes
any leftover clay back into the jar.

     How do you feel?

I rub my hands together and then feel my arm
where his fingers pressed down.

The   cut   is   gone.
     I search with my fingers,
     trace my skin
     up and down,
     back and forth.
I see a small line,
like the memory of a scratch.

Then it feels like the world
starts to spin cold and warm all at once.
My legs bend and twist.
My grandfather catches me,
sits me in a chair, gets me some water.
What's happening? I ask.
Your body, Etan,
it's experienced something
from another time,
an ancient thing giving its power
to something new right now.

He says this like I should understand what he means.

The world stops spinning.
I feel my feet again,
and I notice something else.
I feel good, strong,
      like I could easily hit a home run
            swinging with just one arm.

Energy

I stand up because I have to move.
My legs want to run, but most of all
I feel my insides swirling,
 full of words,
  maybe all the words
  I've kept inside for the past few months
  suddenly desperate to get out.
I want to talk about Malia,
about missing Jordan,
Mom.

I pace around the shop, my words spilling out,
and my grandfather laughs trying to keep up
with everything I'm saying.
Etan! He stands up.
You feel good? Yes?
I nod. He grabs my shoulders, looks me in the eyes.
Grandpa, what did you do?

Confession

The clay from this jar
is from an even more ancient place,
given to me by my father,
your great-grandfather.
It's been in our family for generations.
It's clay, Etan, from the Holy Land,
from generations ago
before our family even came to Prague.

This is the last of it,
and this, too. He points to the other jar.
This is all that remains.
It came with us in this box,
one of the few things we could carry when we had to flee.
I've heard the stories before, but now they are coming to life.

The Clay That Heals

My grandfather sits down heavily in his chair.
    I am getting older, Etan.
    All of us who came
    on that voyage are getting older.
He rests his heavy hand on his chest
like he usually does when the coughing is bad.
    I want to be here with you
    through this hard time.

I notice that he isn't coughing
right now. His voice smooth,   clear.

This ancient clay
    is from the Dead Sea,
        Etan,   *it can heal.*

In the silence I feel my arm where the cut was.
    Yes, a few drops of clay
        may bring wholeness into your body.
      I have to ask him:
So you mean you won't have to cough anymore?

    Etan, he says,
    until today, I resisted using it.
He looks down,
and I see tears, his face red.
    I tried it before on someone else,
    and for a little while it was a miracle.
I look at him. *Grandma?* I say softly.
Yes,   *but*   *it lasted*   *only a short time,*
    and when it didn't last,
    I think it was the hardest
    on your father.

Since then, he's had
a hard time trusting
his faith. I don't like it,
but I understand.

The change is real—
we transform one way or another—
but it is not always permanent, Etan.
Her pain returned.
She seemed at peace, but I was not.
I swore from then on to try to be thankful for what I had,
to remember the words of the Talmud.

The one to whom the miracle is happening does not recognize
the miracle.

I hoped too much in the clay.
I forgot the greater power,
the true miracle
is in the way we are made to be who we are.

But it's getting worse for me,
my coughing, so here I am again
and just maybe this might heal my cough,
to make me strong for a little while longer.

He looks tired
holding the jar in his hands.
I put my arms
            around his
                    broad shoulders
        and whisper,
                Todah, Grandpa. Thank you.

NL West (Sunday, Oct. 1)

They did it!
My father bursts in the shop,
his hands black with dried roofing tar.
The Giants lost to the Padres, but they're still in first!
He grabs me tightly,
lifts me up, and spins me around.
He smells like he's worked all day.
We're going to the National League Championships
Wednesday night against the Cubs.
I think we got this.

He sets me down,
takes a breath, looks around.
Hey, he says. *What's all this?*
His eyes lock with my grandfather's,
his hands slowly ball into fists.
He walks to where
        the jars
            sit side by side,
and for a while
no one says anything,
the dim light of the jewelry shop
sitting heavily on the three of us.
I feel the words in my body,
still strong, working their way
out of me like they haven't for such a long time.
    Dad, it's okay,
    Grandpa was showing me
    all of this stuff . . .

My father's eyes grow large
and he puts his hand to his mouth,
like he can't believe it.

I haven't seen that jar
since I . . .
since Ma . . .
But he stops there.
I see a tear in the corner of his eye.
He shakes it off.
You know, I tried to use some of that clay once.
When I was a kid, younger than you,
some of the other kids in my school
told me that my dad was a "dirty immigrant,"
called me names for being Jewish.
Your grandfather talked to the school,
the school talked to their parents,
but nothing helped.
So I took the clay from the box.
      My eyes get wide.
I actually tried to make a golem.
I wanted it to protect us from those bullies
the way it did in your grandfather's stories.

I used almost all the clay,
tried to make the golem
on the front stoop of our building.
You know what happened?

My grandfather walks closer to him.
My father takes a step back.

It rained,
and the clay washed away down the street.

Services

My grandfather finally speaks.
Remember we have services tomorrow.
Rabbi Rosenthal expects us.
My father looks down.
Pop, I have to work, and you know how I feel.
None of this, he waves his arm at the box, and the jars,
is for me anymore.
My grandfather looks at him, and then at me.
> *Hasn't it been long enough?*
> > *You don't just stop your life.*
> > > *She would want you to go.*
I think he's talking about my mom,
or maybe my grandmother.
I need the money, Pop.
> *Besides, all the games are on.*

Oy gevalt! my grandfather groans,
and turns away.

Everyone's Talking

At school everyone talks about baseball.
Since what happened with Jordan,
I've spent most recesses drawing,
but I feel a little different today.
So I sit at the usual table with Jordan and some of the other kids.
Martin is telling everyone about the A's.
Rickey Henderson will kill the Giants if we play them.
They are way too slow.
The A's will totally win.
They argue,   get loud,   too loud.
I remember quiet days
sorting our baseball cards into team lineups.

Then Martin turns to me.
What do you think, Etan?
I feel my stomach drop.
Everything that's in my head washes away like water
down a toilet bowl.
I try . . .
I want to run away
but that would be worse.
        I find my bareket in my pocket, take it out,
                    wrap my fingers around it,
                                squeeze.
Martin looks at me. *What's that?* he says.
Then, with fastball speed
he reaches into my hand and pulls the stone right out of it.
Is this your pet rock? He laughs and shows it to the others.
Jordan looks over.
        C'mon, Martin, cut it out.
I reach for it. He pulls it away.

Then from somewhere deep,
        somewhere even ancient,
            I grab his wrist as tight as I can and growl,
            GIVE IT BACK!
At first he tries to pull away,
but when he hears me,
        his fist loosens,
                he drops
                        the stone into my hand.
C'mon, let's go play ball, he says.
They get up to spend the rest of lunch playing baseball.
Jordan looks over. *You want to play, Etan?*
Martin cuts in, *Of course he doesn't.*
He can't hit anyway.

An Unexpected Companion

I promised Malia a pumpkin.
So right after school
I rush toward Main Street to get one from Mrs. Li.
But on the way, I remember Buddy.

Mrs. Hershkowitz is there, hanging out her third-story window.
Etan! she yells. *Etan, ETAN!*
I look up, think about telling her I can't do it today.
ETAN! Buddy needs you. My back is killing me, Etan.
She says my name in every sentence.
Buddy gets inside the basket, his tail wagging
as he's lowered to me. He jumps up, and I grab the leash.
        I get an idea.
Mrs. Hershkowitz? But it's not loud enough.
WHAT?
I try again. *CAN I TAKE BUDDY with me?*
She nods, waves, ducks inside.
I can't wait for Malia to meet Buddy!

Buddy in the Shop

I stop at the bakery, get the everything bagel
loaded with cream cheese for my grandfather.
He sits at his workbench with the giant loupe over his eye
looking deeply into a watch.
He's coughing again, trying to stay steady.
When he hears the dog, he looks up. *Buddy!*
Buddy spins around, all tail and tongue
and feet scratching on the wood floor.

> *How are you doing?*
I hold up the pumpkin. *Buddy is coming with me.*
> *Well you better get going,*
> *the days are getting shorter.*

I see the treasure box on the shelf.
I think about the clay, my arm gets cold,
I smell wet earth in my nostrils like a sudden breeze.

Grandpa, there's clay in the stream behind Malia's house.
Do you think that clay might be magic, too?

He looks at me, pets the dog,
lowers his cup of tea,
lets Buddy take a drink,
which makes him sneeze.

> *Who am I to say?*
> *Sometimes the old world and the new world*
> *are just the same place at different times.*
> *Maybe, Etan.*

I empty my backpack except for the notebook
and make room for a pumpkin.

Dogs

At the dragon mailbox
I try to keep Buddy from marking his territory.
No cars in the driveway this time.
When we reach the door, Malia opens it wide,
sings, *I will be waiting* . . . ,
Blankie wrapped around her face like a scarf.
When Buddy sees her he leaps with all four paws
right into her arms.
Who's this little one?
She lifts him high, and Buddy licks her face.
I tell her about Buddy and Mrs. Hershkowitz.
He's so adorable!
She shuts the door behind her.
Here, let's take him down to our secret place?
Okay, I say, *but I also* . . .
I unzip my backpack.
Ohhhh, you remembered!

She stops at a garden shed
on the side of the house
and pulls out two small
folding knives. Holds them up. *For carving!*

Down the Path

The afternoon light is darker than last time;
the trees reach higher, cast more shadows on the path.
Malia carries Buddy, but then we hear something
move through the bushes below.
He leaps out of her arms, charges down the path,
dirt flying behind him,
until he disappears into the green.

Pumpkin Carving

Buddy! Buddy!
We hear him barking, feet shuffling through brush,
and eventually he blunders into the clearing
next to the water.
I set the backpack down near the Sitting Stones.

Buddy's face and paws are covered in dirt
like he's discovered it for the very first time.

Let's carve!
Malia unfolds the knives, hands one to me.
I've never carved a pumpkin on my own.
We set it between the stones,
and Malia slices into the orange flesh.
Ewwwww, she laughs. *Dig in.*

We take turns scooping seeds and pumpkin guts
into an orange pile.
Buddy licks at the guts, gnaws a little on the seeds, spits them out.

I notice her arms are more red than usual,
even some red scratch marks scabbed over.

So are you going to sing at the talent show?
I quietly ask.
*Mayybeee. I want to, but I don't think
        my mom and dad will let me.*

We wash our hands off in the water.
It's going to be dark soon.
I didn't think I would stay today.

She can't stop scratching,
her fingers running on her arm.
    Stop staring, she yells.

We finish the pumpkin,
hold it up against the light filtering through the trees.
Yay! She smiles. We set it down,
and I notice a dark smudge on Blankie,
her arm bare, open, it's bleeding where her scratching
rubbed it raw.

Smoothing It Over

Are you okay Malia? I ask.
    Fine. I'm fine.
She walks to the pool,
splashes water on her arm.

I kneel down at the edge of the pool.
Buddy lies down between us;
his brown-and-white head nestles into his paws.

I wanted to tell you about something that happened, I say.
I tell her about my grandfather,
about clay and ancient things,
how the scratch on my arm almost completely disappeared.
Maybe, I say, scooping the clay from the bottom of the pool,
lifting its reddish-brown gooeyness out of the water,
Maybe this can help you?
    Maybe here,
                where trees can talk,
                    the clay is magic, too.

She stares into the water,
and I notice that her blanket is lowered now, around her shoulders,
her face still swollen on the side.

    I don't know, Etan.
    If there's magic clay in the water,
    how come I don't know about it?

There have been ancient magical items
in my grandfather's shop all these years, and I didn't know.

    What do I do? she asks.
Ummm, just something like this.

I take the clay in my hand,
and I splash it down on her arm,
but I miss and some of the clay splatters onto Buddy,
     who yelps, repositions himself.

I try again, slowly this time.
I spread the clay in circles,
and I put one hand
over her heart and close my eyes.
I don't know what to say,
so I recite the prayer for bread at Shabbat.
     Baruch ata Adonai, Eloheinu Melech ha-olam, hamotzi
     lechem min ha'aretz.
     Nothing happens at first, but then,
     Etan, she cries, *it feels . . .*
         itchy   *ITCHY!*
She grits her teeth, pushes her hair behind her ears.
I don't know Etan,   *it's reaalllly itchy.*
Then, all at once, she plunges her arm into the pool
and circles it in the cloudy water.

By the time she takes it out,
Buddy gets up, starts to lick her arm,
and she giggles until anything that
was supposed to happen fades into the evening.

Allergies

It's getting dark.
We set the pumpkin on the porch.
I'll get a candle! She runs inside.
Just then, her mom pulls into the driveway;
I wave, but I see she has a strange look.
Etan, she says, closing the car door.
What is that dog doing here?
I look at her, and suddenly every word that bubbled up
immediately pops.
*Malia's allergic to dogs, this will make her skin
flare up even more.*
Her voice
     like cymbals clashing
              over my ear.

Malia comes out
with Lola behind her.

Malia, you know better than to play with a dog!
I'm sorry Momma, Malia whispers.
It's my fault, I think.
Change your clothes right now.
Keep this dog outside.
Let's call your dad.
I find a word,
       Sorry.
Mrs. Agbayani looks at me,
her eyes turned down, shakes her head, walks inside.
That's when I let myself cry.

Waiting

Lola gives us each a slice of toast
with coconut jam spread across the top.

Malia sits with me on the porch,
waiting for my dad to come,
but Buddy has to stay by the mailbox.

I'm sorry Malia, I say.
       It's okay. You didn't know.
       There's lots of things you don't know about me.
I look at our pumpkin;
the small candle burns brighter.
She reaches over, punches me in the shoulder.
       So if I do the talent show,
       will you help me?
            Can you maybe come over tomorrow?
       I need an audience.

I think so, I say.
Do you think your mom will let me?

From far away I see the high headlights of the truck,
its engine loud on the quiet road.
Malia walks me to the mailbox,
sneaks in one more face lick from Buddy.
Who knows, she says, looking at her arm.
Maybe the clay IS magic.

Trouble

I get in the truck,
Buddy jumps up into my lap.
Do I need to tell you how worried we were?
You're supposed to be at the shop.
Not to mention that Mrs. Hershkowitz
is worried about her dog.
Somehow, without thinking too much,
I feel the words passing through my lips. *I'm sorry,*
we were carving pumpkins,
and   I   forgot.
I start crying again even though I try not to.
My father looks over.
      Oh, don't cry.
      You're getting older, Etan,
      crying isn't always the way.
My father puts his hand in my hand.

The moon is out,
and the trees bend terrible
shadows along Forest Road,
and just before we turn,
he looks at me.

They call her the creature?
Why? She doesn't look bad at all.

Tuesday

I crunch cereal, try to finish my math homework.
I don't mind doing homework, but lately,
it's been hard.
My mom was usually the one to sit with me
in case I had any questions.
But now I do it on my own.

Tonight's the night.
Dad sounds like a game show announcer.
Game 1, Giants at Cubs!
Wrigley Field is far away,
but don't worry, it's available right here.
He waves his arm around the room, fluffs a pillow.
Dad, I say, *I promised Malia*
I would help her practice for the talent show.

He looks at me. *Listen, that's fine.*
He puts his rough hands on both my shoulders.
I'll tell your grandfather,
but you need to be home on time.
Ride your bike from now on,
          and . . .
He looks at me, reaches into his back pocket.

Don't tell your grandfather yet,
it's on the Sabbath, and I don't want an argument,
but my boss gave us tickets to Game 4!
Saturday at Candlestick!

I drop my book, stand up,
hug my dad.
He sings, "Take Me Out to the Ball Game,"
shoves breakfast bowls into the sink.
And then I remember something.
I pull the river picture from the notebook,
take an envelope from the drawer,
        fold the picture
                and put it inside.
Slowly I write out
the address on the refrigerator,
and I draw a heart in the corner.
        Mail this to Mom?

Singing Practice

It's colder today.
Fall is setting in, and the fog, thicker now.
More and more pumpkin faces fill the dark windows.
On my bike, I get to Malia's faster than ever
and she's waiting for me at the door.
>   *I don't have a lot of time,*
>   *I have to—*
Great! she says.
Hands me her boom box and a backpack.
She wraps Blankie around her face like a hood,
and we head down the forest path.

We put the silver boom box on a Sitting Stone.
When I say so press play, okay?
She bows to the trees,
spins once
>   all the way around.
>   I'm sure today
>   of all days
>   they are listening.

Now.

She points at me.
I press play, and the drumbeats
and keyboard pops fill the space near the pool,
the water rippling.

She sings.
>   *If you're lost you can look*
>   *and you will find me . . .*
To the tree, the pool, the afternoon sky.

I feel the music go through me,
her voice floating across the water in the pool,
filtering through the knotty branches,
humming in the Sitting Stones.

At the end,
she bows and Blankie falls over her head.
     She stands up,
          blows the hair out of her face.
Her face seems redder, too, swollen.
Scratch marks across her neck
          that I didn't see before.

Well? she says,
     wrapping Blankie back around.

For some reason,
     even now when I want to talk,
          the words won't come out,
so I hesitate,
     not on purpose,
          but by now
     I know
          that silence
              can wound,
and by the time
     I muster the words
              it was good,
     it's too late.
I see her face change,
     eyes turned down,
          tears already on the way.

The Argument

Why didn't you like it?
She stomps in the dirt, presses stop on the boom box.
I . . .
  Oh what, you can't talk today?
No . . . *I* . . .
    This is a stupid idea anyway.
She wraps Blankie tighter and walks off toward the trees.
I see her hands at her neck
scratching,
her fingers wild on her skin.

I squeeze the stone in my pocket,
it doesn't help. For a second
I think of the clay in the pool;
if I smeared it on my face
said just the right word,
would that work?
Malia, it was so good.
  You are so good.

Silence.

I think the trees liked it, too.

She spins,
    her dark hair
        opens like wings.

    Oh, suddenly you have words?
    You can't talk to the trees;
    how do you know they liked it?

I don't know why, Malia . . .
    Yes, you do, she says. *I think you can always talk!*

Her voice grows louder.
　　　You just don't want to!

I squeeze the stone in my pocket.
She scratches the skin on her neck.

I feel it in my belly,
words swirl.

Well, you should STOP SCRATCHING!

She looks at me, her teeth clenched.
　　　Oh, did you squeeze your little green stone hard
　　　enough to yell?

I take the bareket out of my pocket,
run a finger over its smooth green edges, hold it up to her face.
This? I feel anger in deep wells
boiling up from my toes.
I don't even need this stupid thing.
And then,
without thinking,
I throw it　　　　far　　　　into the stream,
watch it bounce
　　　　　　rock to rock
down
　　　into
　　　　　　the water.

　　　Etan!
We both go after it,
slipping on moss-covered stones,
searching in the shallows,
but we can't find it.
　　　Can't find it anywhere.

Losing Control

Sometimes losing something
helps you find what you are really looking for.

>   *Sorry, Etan*, Malia says.
> *No, I'm sorry*, I reply.
> We walk with wet feet and tired hearts.
>   I carry the boom box.
> *You do sound really good.*

She smiles.
I can tell she's trying not to scratch.
>   *It's hard, okay?*
>   *My dad says it comes from worry.*
>   *It doesn't matter. It's just how I am.*
>   *It comes and goes;*
>   *I can't control it.*

If I could never scratch,
I wouldn't.
If you could speak
the way you wanted to . . .
She stops,
looks up the hill at the fog rolling in.

Maybe, she says,
you should
shove some of that clay
in your mouth,
you know,   *to heal it?*

>   We laugh.

>   *Maybe YOU should*
>   *cover your whole body*
>   *so you look like a golem.*

She walks to the pool,
scoops some clay into her hands.
Can you imagine me at school?
I really would be "the creature."

She curls her fingers to a claw,
pretends to scratch her face.
     It might mess up class,
      everyone making fun of me.

I don't know.
We reach the top of the hill.
Lots of kids do weird stuff,
maybe they can't control it either.

Until

She stops at the edge of the clearing.
You know why they call me that?
    The creature?
A long time ago,
my parents finally let me go to the school.
But so many kids made fun of me,
pointing at my eye and the way my hands
never stopped scratching.
They called me "the creature,"
told everyone to stay away or they might get it, too.
I told my parents I wanted to be homeschooled again,
but my mom had just started back to work,
and they didn't think it could be so bad.
    Until.
She looks at her arms,
touches her fingers to her face.
You probably don't remember.
We sang at the assembly.
I loved singing,
but my dress was so itchy.
She rubs her arms
like she can feel it now.
So I did what any little kid would do.
    I scratched, scratched,
        scratched, right there on stage,
my arms and hands everywhere.
    My parents believed me after that,
and I haven't been to school ever since.

It Gets Worse

In the afternoons
we go to the Sitting Stones,
and while her singing gets better every day,
her skin gets worse—
red bumps, hives on her legs,
her face swollen until her eye almost shuts.

But she sings,
and I doodle,
draw maps of the trees,
and fog sits in the forest.

I can't come this weekend, I say.
*It's Shabbat and the High Holidays,
and we're supposed to go to synagogue all the time.*

    What's Shabbat?

In my mind I picture
the brisket my mom used to make
and challah twisted into hearts,
with honey dripping from wood spoons,
roasted chicken with dried fruit,
brownies or halva for dessert.
I tell her about all of it,
my mouth watering.
    Wow, she says.
*But since my mom left,
we usually eat my grandpa's chili
or something simple.*

    Is that why you don't like to talk, Etan?

I look at her.

> *I mean maybe you let your mom*
> *take all your words with her?*
> *I mean maybe she's the one you talked*
> *to the most, and now that she's . . .*
> *well, maybe you just don't want to give them*
> *to anyone else?*
> *I mean besides your grandpa or even your dad sometimes.*

I look at her.
She wraps Blankie around her head a bit
but then smiles big.

> *I mean, until now, of course?*
What?
> *Me, dummy! Now you have me.*
> *Maybe you just needed a friend who wants to hear*
> > *what you have to say.*

She scratches her neck, walks to the pool.

You should come sometime, I say. *To Shabbat, I mean.*
> *Okay*, she says,
wading into the water.

> > *For now, I'm gonna find that darn green rock.*

Agreements

After the Shabbat candles are lit,
Mrs. Hershkowitz feeds Buddy bits of challah
beneath the table.
She winks at me to do it, too.
Across from us my grandfather is shaking
his head at my father.

> *Listen, son, I love baseball as much as anyone,*
> *but it's the High Holidays and this is not right.*

Pop, once in a lifetime,
don't you see?
The series is tied 1–1 . . .

> And on like this,
> > until my grandfather
> > > puts a giant hand
> > > > over the hand of my father.

> *Fine, we'll go,*
> *but promise me,*
> > *promise me*
> > > *you won't miss Yom Kippur service on*
> > > *Sunday.*

He smiles at Mrs. Hershkowitz,
but she's dipping challah into honey,
letting Buddy lick it off.
Fine, Pop, yes, of course I will.

Baseball Game

Even from our seats at the top of Candlestick Park,
we feel the energy from sixty thousand people
shouting and cheering with every single play.

My father is alive,
standing more than sitting
every time Clark comes to the plate.
The game is so close.
Runs in the first inning,
the crowd singing
      or shouting bad words
           when the score is tied.
      For me, it's loud,
thousands of untuned musical instruments
trying to play together.
My grandfather puts his arm around me.
Wonderful game. Do you miss playing?
I don't know how to answer this.
I'm sure there's a reason.
I want to say,
      I just don't.
But that's never the right answer for grown-ups.

Soft Pretzels

I feel for the stone in my pocket.
    Grandpa?
He leans in to listen.
    I lost the green stone.

The Cubs get a run in the top of the seventh,
so the crowd suddenly tightens in a deep breath.

My grandfather puts his arm around my shoulders.
Etan, I want a soft pretzel.
You want one?

Words Come Out

Extra salt,
crispy and soft all at the same time.
We go to get mustard,
and that's when we see him,
holding his own pretzel—
Jordan, wearing a blue kippah,
his father standing just behind.

My grandfather hugs Jordan.
    Shana Tovah! A good year!
And they talk about how important
the game is, and that they had to come
even though it's Saturday.
Hey, Etan, Jordan says.
I try to say hi.
    I can't.

I got my Ken Holtzman card finally.
Did you know he's Jewish, too?
This is such a good game.
If the A's beat the Blue Jays tomorrow, they go to the Series!
    I smile.
You should play baseball again at school.
Martin's got a big mouth but he's all talk.

The grown-ups say their goodbyes,
then my grandfather looks at me with pleading eyes.
    J-or-dan? I say.
It feels like a whole galaxy of time
before the words come out.
    You guys should come over
    for Shabbat sometime.

He smiles.
That's a great idea, I can bring my cards!

By the time we get back, Candlestick is vibrating
because the Giants scored two runs to pull ahead
       all the way
             until the end of the game.
And then later, for two more games
       after that
       all the way
             into the 1989 World Series.

Part

4

Sunday Morning

I ride my bike down to Main Street.
Mr. Cohen's bakery is full of Sunday people
    wearing Sunday clothes
        but with Giants hats,
            and kids carrying pennants and
            baseball gloves.
I get in line to buy my grandfather
        his coffee and bagel,
            a last meal
before he starts his Yom Kippur fast,
leading up to the day of atonement.
It's a time, he explains, *to say sorry*
for things we've done
and mean it.
A time for forgiveness
and fate.
It's also twenty-five hours of not eating anything!
But when Mr. Cohen sees me,
his head bobbing from behind the counter,
he waves at me. *Etan, Etan!*
I push through the crowd,
    ducking under,
        slipping through.
and he pulls me around.
Etan, I am so swamped. Can you PLEASE take these
donuts to Grace Covenant Community Center?
I will never get them there in time.
He hands me two pink boxes.
There's a jelly for you and bagels for your grandpa
when you get back.

Sign-up Sheet

There are people going to church,
the community center,
kids carrying kites, walking dogs.
I think about how long it's been since we went to temple.
We should be going later today, but I wonder if my father
actually will.

Outside, I see the Covenanteers passing out programs for the day,
and in the doorway a long red banner:

HARVEST FESTIVAL
TALENT SHOW
AND SPAGHETTI SUPPER

Etan! They call me over.
I hold up the donut box, and they bring me inside.
So, Etan, will you be joining us for the talent show?
The Covenanteer holds up a clipboard full of names and acts:
singers, piano players,
Hula-Hoopers, ventriloquists, at least ten magicians.
I hold the pencil, think about Malia
singing beneath the trees.
Then I sign her name, unsure of the spelling.

Clay

I get back to the shop
with the bagels and coffee.
Grandpa's there with the loupe over his eye,
holding a watch.

     Etan, I am so behind.
     Thank you for the coffee.

I sit at the workbench.
Grandpa, Malia is singing in the talent show.
I slide the red paper over to him.
Next Tuesday at 4!
He examines it.

     She agreed to this?

Kind of?
But there might be a baseball game.
He stops what he is doing,
sets everything down.

     Etan, I noticed
     when you talk about your friend,
     your words come out just fine.

I nod.
It's just that her skin is getting worse,
and she is always scratching until it bleeds.
He puts down the loupe, sips coffee.

     Tell me more.

An Idea

I tell him everything.
Mrs. Li even gave her herbs
and some kind of goji berry tea,
but her skin
> *just stays*
>> *the same.*
Grandpa, is there a stone we can give her?
Or something else?

He thinks for a while, looks at the treasure box.

> *The old and the new sometimes struggle*
> *to work together.*
>> *Everything is always changing,*
>>> *but maybe I do have something.*

He gets up and carries the treasure box over.
As he opens the box, I smell earth, and wood;
it's spicy in my nose.
He pulls out the jars of clay, reaches in deeper,
opens a small leather pouch, and pours smooth stones
into his hand.
He lays them all on the table.

Grandpa, maybe,
I mean, what about the clay?
My heart races.

You said the golem comes to protect us in our greatest need?
He looks at me.
> *This is not the same, and besides, you know,*
> *there is not enough clay for the golem to come alive.*
I guess it makes sense.

We don't need a guardian; what we need is a miracle.
And even with the clay from the Dead Sea,
there is just not enough.
I think about the pool in our secret place.
Grandpa, wait.
What if we took some of OUR clay,
the healing clay from the Dead Sea,
and mixed it with some of the clay from the stream?

He pulls the jars close to him.
I can tell he's thinking.

He raises his hands,
his eyes wide now.
We shouldn't risk it.
We just don't know if her pain will come back even
worse.
He puts a fist on the table. His voice grows louder.
No, it's one thing, for OUR family,
but to bring others into it
is very dangerous. No.

I feel my stomach tighten.
I'm mad.
Mad at him,
the words boiling up.
But what's it for, then?
Is it supposed to stay in that jar forever?

My grandfather leans back,
his eyes at first like fire.
But then, cool, and soft again.

Well, that's the boy I know.
But I still think the clay is not the answer.

He digs into the leather pouch,
pulls out a small blue stone.

    Ah, this is what I was looking for.
    Sapphire. Take this,
    it may help her feel peace.

He smiles at me, puts the jars back in the box.

    You should go, he says.
    I'm sure she feels better
    when you are there.
    But be back for services!

I look again at the box,
imagine the weight of the jars in my hands.
    What if I just put them in my backpack?
    Mixed the ancient clay with the newer clay?

What if we tried?

Mrs. Li

...waits for me outside the shop.
She walks over, hands me a brown bag.

Good morning, Etan. Take this.
It's more tea with different herbs.
        Thank you, I say. *I hope it works.*
Etan, she says, *it's nice to hear your voice again.*
I take the bag, and as much as I try, I can't resist.
When I open it, my insides get tight.
The smell is so strong.

Mrs. Li nods.
It's okay, Etan.
This tea recipe is my mother's.
It helped soothe so many of us
on long, cold days at sea.
It may smell funny to you, but it's strong, I promise you.
I try not to use my nose,
but now the smell is trapped there.

Etan, never forget this.
Mrs. Li folds the bag closed.
Your friendship for this girl is the oldest
and strongest form of medicine you can ever give her.
        Remind her that she is not alone.

Tremor

I ride up the hill.
Already the fog is coming in along Forest Road.
Near the first redwoods, crows caw together in high branches,
then suddenly fall silent,
spread their dark wings
      against the gray-and-white sky,
take off fast.

BOOOOM.

The noise is like a cannon shot
or a jet flying low.
But the crows are the only things in the sky.
The bike jumps like I ran into a hole.

BOOOOM.
The trees sway, then jerk in one direction
like the whole earth sneezed.

She Gets Worse

Outside on the porch
Malia is folded over, quietly crying
in her mother's lap.
I wonder if the earthquake scared her again?
Mrs. Agbayani looks at me, tears in her own eyes.
She puts her arm out to me.
I walk toward her until her hand
on my shoulder pulls me tightly in.

Blankie is spread evenly over Malia's body,
but I can see her legs, red, swollen,
hives like scales.

Without moving even an inch
I hear her voice like it's right in my ear.
        It got worse.
Her voice is stuffed into her nose
and it sounds funny,
so I can't help but laugh just a little.
And that's when she looks up,
her face more red than I've ever seen,
her one eye swollen, but with the other
she glares at me.
     I shrink
           inside the orb of her eye.
She gives me an angry smile
           her head in her heads.

Mrs. Agbayani exhales.
It's a new outbreak, Etan, worse than we've seen before.
The eczema is spreading.
     I hold up the tea. *I have this from Mrs. Li.*

Malia's body constricts.
　　　Ahhhh, I can smell it from here!
Mrs. Agbayani takes the bag,
holds it arm's-length away.

I'll take it inside.
Malia leans forward, her head resting sideways.

It's on my back, and it hurts to sit up.

I don't know what to say, and this time
it has nothing to do with finding my words.

Whatever you do DON'T say anything.
Can we just go down to the forest?
　　　She slowly stands,
　　　　　　her shoulders hunched.

What the Trees Say

She stops at each tree,
       rests her forehead on the rough trunks,
whispers words in Tagalog.

So what are the trees saying? I ask.
She leans against one of them.
       They say something big is coming.
That seems obvious.
Of course it is, I say. *I mean the World Series, and . . .*
       Malia turns to me. No, *dummy, trees don't care about
       baseball.*
       It's something else. These earthquakes . . .
       it's like the earth calling out, speaking a new language.
       The trees are trying to understand it.
We slowly wind our way to where the Sitting Stones
sleep in the mist by the pool.

My words spill out.
I signed you up today for the talent show. Next Tuesday!
       She sighs. *Etan, look at me.*
       You think I am ready to get up in front of people?
       I never go anywhere, not even school.
              What was I thinking?
She walks to the pool and looks in,
her face shining in the wavy water.
       Look at me.
       I mean, I AM a creature.
She scratches her neck, and then her legs.
They start to bleed.
She tries to reach the middle of her back.

I walk over, but she waves me away,
smashes both hands into the water,
then *SPLASH* again, soaking Blankie.
She reaches deep into the pool,
pulls up handfuls of clay,
squeezes it
until it oozes between her fingers.

> *I don't want this.*
> *I don't want any of this.*

She drops her hands into the water,
watches the clay swirl in the cloudy wet.

That's when I make the decision.

Hope

Sometimes I imagine
that the words in my mind
fall into my belly,
swim in my dark, empty insides.
But lately, even the dark places
seem to be filling up with enough light.
My words can't hide anymore.

*I have to go! I have to get back for services and
        because if the Giants and A's win,
they go to the Series.*

Malia stands, rubbing her arms,
Blankie over her head like a lion's mane
as we walk up the hill over to my bike.

What services? Malia asks.
        Oh, it's Yom Kippur, I say.
        *It's when we think about atonement,
        all the bad things we've done.
        Like a chance to make things right.
        Grown-ups have to fast.
        I don't have to. Not yet.*

Malia smiles. *Sounds kind of nice.*
I wave, pedal off.
She yells,
        I am NOT drinking the tea!

Baseball Mitt

When I get home,
it's almost time for services.
My father is on the couch in his Candy Maldonado jersey
with a shining bowl of peanuts and boxes of Cracker Jacks,
baseball cards
everywhere, his Louisville Slugger in his hand.
He throws me my mitt. It hits me in the chest.
    Ow.
No time for ow!
Both games are on! Put on your mitt.
      But Dad? I say. *We promised Grandpa ...*

Services

When my grandfather comes to the door he's dressed in white,
his face shining, his hand on his belly.
Ready for synagogue?
The meal and then Kol Nidre?
But we are not, and he can tell.
I suddenly feel hollow,
torn in half,
like we forgot something we were supposed to do.
My grandfather
        looks at me,
                looks at my father.
        You promised.
Then louder. *YOU PROMISED.*
I know, Pop, but . . .   *NO,*   my grandfather yells.
This is Yom Kippur.
This is our time to make things right in our hearts,
and you keep watching baseball?
Your wife is away in a mental hospital
and you think being here is best?
And then, all at once, he starts coughing.

I get him some water.
He sips. Turns to my father.
This beautiful boy
needs to be back in shul.
It's been long enough;
his bar mitzvah is coming!
What will we do?

        My father hangs his head
        and I know that look.
        He's searching for words
        he can't find.

This is who we are, my grandfather continues,
how we've stayed strong through everything that's happened.
Don't give up, not now.
What are we made of?
We do not give up.

My grandfather stands,
hands me his water glass.
It's time for a change.
And he walks out.

Tears and Snot and Everything

I don't understand everything about Yom Kippur,
but ever since I was little we dressed up,
went to services all together.
      This is where I remember her the most,
      the green eyes of my grandmother,
      her checkered dress and fuzzy hat,
      her strong hands around my cheeks.
      I was so little,
      but I can still feel them.

My father lets out deep breaths,
shoulders falling.
Etan, listen.
And I can't help it,
maybe it's the thought of my grandmother,
or the hole in the apartment where my mother should be,
or the thought of letting my grandfather down,
or maybe something holier or more sacred
that I don't understand,
but I start to cry in a way that I haven't for a while,
tears and snot and everything.

My father drops his mitt,
puts his arms around me until the tears stop.
      I know, son, but he has to understand,
      I mean . . . once in a liftetime!
But he knows it's not just about baseball.
      I just . . . since your grandmother died,
      and now with your mom,
      it's hard for me to go to synagogue without them.

He holds me there,
and I hold him,
then we quietly watch the game.

By the time the sun is completely set,
the A's are going to the World Series,
and the Giants have one more game.

When We Don't Go

In the morning, my father is humming at the table,
but it's not about the big game.
Instead I see his open prayer book.
Maybe we will go to services today.
It feels like we should go.
I want a chance to atone, to make things right,
to start again.

I sit down across from him.
He's holding a photo in his hand.
It's the three of us, standing at Fort Point
beneath the Golden Gate Bridge.
The sun is shining, the water is bright blue behind the red bridge.

He looks up at me,
wet eyes and scraggly beard,
like he's been stuck thinking for days.
I'm sorry, Etan.
And he takes my hand.
I'm doing my best. I promise.
One day soon we will go back.

I believe him.

Giants Win

Will Clark drives in the final run
with a single down the center.
My father sweeps me into his arms, spins me around!

All of Main Street dances shop to shop
waving pennants, streaming rolls of paper across streetlights.
Confetti popcorns into the air.
Firecrackers and sparklers crackle and shine like a parade.
The A's verses the Giants, the battle of the bay,
is about to happen!

A "Half-Open Door"

After a while, things calm down.
My grandfather isn't back from services yet.
I ask my father if I can have a key to the shop and wait there
where it's quieter.
He barely looks, just hands me the key.

Outside I see Mrs. Li weaving between
excited baseball people on the street.
She cleans pumpkin guts,
exploded tomatoes,
and smashed eggplant.
I unlock the door to the shop, grab the broom,
and I help sweep ruined fruit into compost buckets.
It takes forever, and it's getting darker,
long after sunset now;
my grandfather must be coming back soon.
And even though the world
has become a baseball game,
I still have to go to school tomorrow.

　　　So much mess, Mrs. Li says.
Thank you, Etan. I stop sweeping. I look at Mrs. Li.
She's always been here,
around us, our whole life.
She used to come sometimes to Shabbat, even Hanukkah.
Mr. Li came here with them all on the *Calypso*.
My grandfather told us that it was hard for him.
Angel Island was different for them.
Mrs. Li said they had a "half-open door,"
where they could see San Francisco
but had to wait for months to be free.

She sometimes talks about poems carved onto the wood walls
by people who had to stay for a long time,
and some who wished they hadn't come at all.
I guess Mr. Li was one of them; he didn't last long.
For Mr. Li,
there were too many ghosts.

Etan, how is Malia?
Worse, I whisper.
Mrs. Li looks at me, stops sweeping,
takes a deep breath,
walks over,
puts her hands
on my shoulders.
I can tell she understands
without needing me to explain,
like my mother would.
Her eyes shine in the streetlights.

What   can we do   for that girl?

Hard Choices

I quietly unlock the door.
I spend so much time here but almost never
without my grandfather.
During the day, the workbench is a mess
of different tools,
    shiny screws,
      books filled with instructions.
But at night, we put every single screw
back in just the right place.
Jars of screws big as your finger and tiny as a flea
set in perfect rows along the wall.

Before my mom went to the hospital,
she told me that sometimes we have to make hard choices,
the kinds that grate against your gut,
that hurt, but you still know
they're the right thing to do.
You have to try,
    have faith,
even if you don't always know what will happen.
What if I bring
    the whole jar of healing clay
      to Malia?
If that clay can help her even for a little while,
      we should use it.
What do we have to lose?
    Is it just supposed to be in a box forever?

This must be one of those hard choices,
because my stomach hurts thinking about taking the jar
even though everything in me
says it's right to help a friend.

The Unexpected Thing

But I can't do it.
I can't take the jar.

I stop at the workbench,
and that's when something unexpected happens.

I see the treasure box on the shelf
    is *already* open,
      the lid lifted, the chains undone.

On the shelf above it
is a canvas bag already packed,
    the jar of clay,
        a note rolled up tied together with twine.

    Here. From behind me,
my grandfather unzips my backpack.
    It's heavy, put it in here.
Grandpa?
He looks younger in his white clothes
    but tired
        from long hours at the synagogue.

    You are right, Etan.
It's been a long day of reflection.
This clay is part of a bigger story of who we are.
It should be for all people.
    We—should be for all people.
When it didn't work on your grandmother, I lost so
much hope,
    but each of us has their own story.
You have a chance to be the light, to help a friend.

This is what it's for.
    He smiles, puts the jar into my pack.

    Mix it with the clay in the stream
    and when you do, say the prayers you know,
    think of good things,
    your mother, this shop, your friend.
        All should be well.
I turn
and his arms are around me.

Are We Golem?

That night before I go to sleep,
I open the notebook to a blank sheet.
I feel the scratch of my pen
against the rough page.
I draw the bubbling stream
pouring into the blue-green pool
near the Sitting Stones.

Then I draw a person, maybe Malia,
going into the water,
and when she comes out she's a golem,
earth-colored, made of clay.

But that doesn't seem completely right.
She's not a creature.
And neither am I.

Like a Holiday

Etan, wake up.
          It's late.
My father nudges me.
I see his tired face, a giant bowl of cereal in his hands.
          We both overslept.
          C'mon, you're gonna be late for school.
Sometimes when we're late he gets mad,
but today he's happy.
Don't worry, he says. *It's like a holiday right now.*
Game 1 is Saturday! Can you believe it?
          Dad?
He takes a huge bite of his cereal.
          Do you think Mom gets to watch the game?
He chews, swallows, smiles.
Of course she does.

He shows me the newspaper, the schedule of games,
starting this weekend.
But then I see the third game, one week away, on Tuesday.
The SAME EXACT day as the talent show!

I decide not to tell him yet.

Phone Call

The phone rings.
Etan, can you?
But he sees my face, remembers.
He leaps to the phone.
Hello? Hi,   I know!   I can't believe it!
Silence as he listens, his face breaking into a smile,
and I know it's my mother.

He looks at me.
Yeah.   Yes.   I will.
Then he says something so quiet
that I can't hear him at all.
He calls me over. I put the phone to my ear,
whisper, *Hello?*
and listen to the delicate
        sound of her voice
                telling me
                        she's coming home
                                soon.

Skipping School

I roll my bike out the front door,
my backpack heavy:
    the notebook, granola bar,
    jar of ancient, magic clay.

I've never skipped school before.
Maybe it's because the world feels so different
or because of some magic
or change, or maybe it's just the excitement
of seeing what might happen.
    Today I have other things to do.

When I reach Malia's house,
the fog is already melting away.
The dragon mailbox is wet with morning dew,
drops of water like slimy scales.

Lola is sitting on the front porch, a huge book in her lap.
She waves at me, gets up, goes inside.
By the time I reach the door,
Malia walks through,
Blankie wrapped fully around her,
a huge textbook in her arms.

Surprise Visit

Etan! Are you in trouble? Are you okay?
Why aren't you in school?
She smiles, and I notice that she's not hiding her face;
it looks a little less swollen.
I lean my bike against the porch, unload the heavy backpack.
I . . . I'm fine, I say.
She looks relieved.

    I'm studying US states.
    Did you know that Georgia is the home of Coca-Cola?
    I mean, I can't drink soda, but . . .
    What's in the backpack?

I lower it to the ground.
I feel so light, like I could fly away.
Can we go to the Sitting Stones? I say.
    Now? she asks.
Yeah!
    Lola! and she goes inside.
I walk up the steps.
    Okay, she said yes,
    but we have to eat first.
She gives us each a plate of chicken adobo
with rice and a fried egg.
I notice that Malia's skin is red and cut in places,
but she isn't scratching.
Maybe the tea is working.
We eat, and she tells me stuff about different states.
    Did you know the Venus flytrap
    is the official plant of North Carolina?
    I bet it could eat our fingers off.

Down the Path

The trees are giants,
sentinels guarding the footpath,
different in the midday light.
Malia touches the trunk of each tree,
and it seems like a whole world is here, something
     I have been missing.
Something that is coming back.

The Jar

When we reach the stones, I blurt it out.
My mom might come home soon!
    That's great, Etan.
She spins around.
So are you feeling better? I ask
Blankie flies in the crisp air.
    A little bit—I mean my skin is red but my eye
    is smaller today.
    But what I want to know is what makes a good,
    shy boy like you
    skip school and come all the way out here?
I open my backpack
and it feels like bolts of gentle lightning
surging through me.
I find the words right away.
I want you to be able to sing.
Malia looks at me for a long time
and for once she's the one who doesn't talk.
People need to know you.
And if she can do it,
then maybe I can do it.

I take the jar out of the bag,
set it on the flat surface of a Sitting Stone.
What is that?
She touches the clay jar, smells it.
        What is this?
            Is this?
Yeah, I breathe out, *it's the real clay,*
my grandfather's clay,
well, his great-great . . .
you know what I mean.
She tries to lift the jar.
    It's heavy, she says.
Yeah.

It's really, really old.
from the Dead Sea.
I try to think about what my grandfather
might say or do here.
So this might make your skin feel better
and a bunch of other stuff.
She nods, quietly whispers,
                    Ooookay . . .
She breathes for a while.
                    Okay. A tear falls down her cheek,
lands on Blankie.
I open the jar, try to think holy thoughts,
fill my head with prayers I know,
fill my mind
        with the sound
            of my grandfather's stories,
                    my mother's voice.
We both peer into the jar.
A small blob of clay sits at the very bottom,
That's it? she says. *Does it smell weird?*
We put our noses close;
it smells like a basement, or a forest floor after a long rain.
I put my finger into the jar, press into the clay.
It smushes down at first, but then it feels like a pin prick.
Ow! I pull it out.
        What? she says, puts her finger in,
and she feels it, too.
        Wow! What is that?
I don't know, I say. *Energy?*
        But there is hardly anything in there.
My grandfather told me we need to mix it with the native clay.
This is your place, your pool, your friends who are trees,
so take some clay from the pool and mix it with the clay
in the jar.

Mixing

Cool, Malia says, and kneels near the pool.
Here goes.
She dips both hands into the water,
scoops clay from the bottom, the water dripping from her hands
as she brings it over.
She scrapes the clay into the mouth of the jar,
    and slowly,
             something happens.
A light mist rises from inside.
We look at each other.
Probably just a temperature change, she says.
I take a pencil from my backpack, and carefully mix the clay
together.
It feels like thick paste.
One clay is pale, milk colored,
the other almost red, like the tree bark.
We watch the colors swirl together,
but they don't blend.
I put the jar on the stone.
Okay, arms first.
She puts her arms forward,
her left is redder, a little swollen.
I put my fingers into the jar.
It's warm, probably from the mixing?
I lift them out,
then in one awkward motion,
trying NOT to let it fall to the ground,
I rub the clay onto her arms,
pressed between my palm and her forearm.
Smear it around!

I can't tell if she's crying, or laughing, she's breathing so fast.
   It's hot. It feels hot.
I remember to pray, to think good thoughts,
my father singing "Take Me Out to the Ball Game,"
ice cream with my mother,
my grandfather's shop,
Jordan stealing a base,
Buddy bouncing in his basket,
and Malia being my friend,
everything
        all at once,
                together,
as I smooth the warm clay over her arms.

The Change

I put more clay on two fingers,
dab it onto her face, around her eye.
I pray,
　　　think of the trees,
the pool, my green bareket, somewhere in the water.
I think of Lola and imagine a Shabbat
with pandesal, coco jam, and lumpia.

When most of the clay is off my hands,
Malia starts humming, her voice like light.
Look! she cries.
Her red, swollen arms
are smooth, clear,
like the red was never there.

　　　I am afraid to move, Malia whispers.
She mouths the words, *What should I do?*
I shrug. *I don't know.*
I cover the jar again.
Do you feel different?
　　　I don't know, yes? No. Yes?
　　　　　I mean yes—
　　　　　　I feel my skin,
　　　　　　　it's my skin!
She runs her fingers over her arms,
put her hands on her face,
pokes it a little.
Could this be?
　　　A real miracle?

What's Next

I go to the pool to clean my hands.
I kneel down, and when I do,
something moves in the earth,
like it's just beneath us.
The water on the pool ripples
like giant raindrops falling,
only there is no rain.
Malia walks over to me.
        Is it an earthquake?
But by the end of her question
it stops.
        What do we do now?
I look around,
the stones,
        the water,
                the trees,
all look the same,
but Malia's face so different,
like she's suddenly more herself.

        Wait! she says.
        Do you think I can keep just a little bit of that clay?

I take the jar back out and unlatch it.
Malia takes a Tic Tac box from her pocket,
and we eat the last few orange Tic Tacs.
Then she fills the tiny, clear container
with clay until it's dark.

        Can you stay for a little while? Malia asks.

I need to get back
but I don't want to be anywhere else.
We sit on the stones together.
She tells me how her dad
comes back from his ship tomorrow.
I tell her about the World Series.
        Then there's even more of a change.
        I put my fingers to my face
        because the swelling in hers has gone down.
        She rubs her hands over her legs, her arms,
        breathing deeply,
        both us trying to feel
                what is real.

Coughing

I get back to the shop,
excited to tell my grandfather
all that happened,
but when I run inside,
I hear him coughing.

Mrs. Li is holding him over the sink,
steam rising around his face,
     hair wet,
          face turned down
               in the mist.
When he finally stops,
he takes a drink of water,
sits in his overstuffed chair,
breathes for a while,
until he sees me there.
     Etan, how did it go?
His words on the edge of a cough.
I take the jar from my backpack.
We mixed it
with the clay in the pool,
it got warm,
we could feel it, Grandpa!
Mrs. Li bends over,
looks my grandfather in the eyes.
Take it slow, Jacob, she says,
then pats me on the head and walks out.
My grandfather smiles.
     Friends, Etan. They are the world. He coughs.
Grandpa, it worked, I think.
I mean, her skin isn't red anymore.
     Well, take each day as it comes.
     Remember, it's a mystery.

He coughs a little more.

> *This town, Etan, is going crazy for baseball,*
> *like there is nothing else*
> *happening in all the world.*

I unlatch the wooden box,
place the jar back inside
next to the other, the golem clay.
Grandpa, there was another tremor today.
> *Did you feel it?*
>> *For a moment*
>>> *I thought maybe it was a golem*
>>>> *rising out of the pool.*

Everything Is Made of Baseball

Game 1 isn't until Saturday,
but Main Street is already a carnival.
Every shop takes sides,
orange banners for the Giants
or green pennants for the A's,
flags in windows
covering Halloween decorations,
like the holiday doesn't even exist.
       Our world is made of baseball.
Even skeletons wear jerseys
and pumpkins wear batters' helmets.
At school, the boys
pull mitts from lockers,
play ball at lunch and recess.
Every day Jordan invites me.
Sometimes I want to, but
when I think about stepping
on the field, it feels
like I have already missed
an important catch,
      or struck out,
          so I don't go.
I feel like one day
I might.

Tickets

When I get home after school,
my father is on the phone with my mother. He's smiling,
and it feels normal,
like sunlight through fog.
Grown-ups
      say what they mean
           by the *way* they say it.
It's not the words,
      it's the noises in between
           that tell the truth.

He hangs up
before he sees me.
      Etan! Look at this.
He goes to the counter
and lifts an uncreased envelope
like it's made of gold.
      This, Etan—my boss came through.
He opens the envelope, and inside
I see the long rectangular tickets,
golden edges, and the words

WORLD SERIES

GAME 3

OCTOBER 17TH, 1989

     We are going to the game!
He lifts me up, spins me around.
But my insides are crumpling,
because of all the dates,
why does it have to be this one?

The date,
        the same date
                as the talent show.

I can't tell him.
            Not yet.
                    What do I do?

Part
5

Practice

For the rest of the week
I ride my bike to Malia's house after school.
She sings "Time After Time,"
> sometimes to Lola and me
> > on an afternoon porch,
> or under old redwoods
> > in our secret place.

One of the days, Malia comes out,
huge pink hair spiked in all directions;
giant star earrings dangle below
and pink painted circles around her eyes
match her pink dress, and even a pink microphone
she made from toilet paper rolls.
Etan! What do you think?
I force myself to say something right away.
> *Wow! Sparkly?*

She puts her hands on her hips. *Wow?*
It's Jem? I'm Jem—you know, and the Holograms?
I thought about what you said,
and I can't wear Blankie, so maybe this?

Each day,
> Malia's skin
> > looks a little better.

Sunlight

On Saturday morning of Game 1,
I ride my bike out to Malia's house
to practice early,
so I have enough time
to get back before the first pitch.
The town is getting ready,
and most of the shops have signs
     CLOSING EARLY—GO GIANTS!
My grandfather says maybe he'll work instead,
that he's got many watches to fix.

The sun is out, the air cool,
and I pedal fast.
I feel like someone else,
someone who can talk
whenever he wants.
My heart feels stronger,
and my mind is clear.
I pedal so hard,
the dirt on the road
makes clouds
in the sunlight behind me.
I round the corner, my head turned
to see the dragon mailbox,
but instead, there's a man there
standing in front,
a steaming cup in his hand.

Her Father

I slow the bike down.
This man,
    dark hair,
        gray in the front,
he smiles.
    So you must be Etan?
His voice is clear, bright.
    Malia has told me about you.
I stand over my bike,
    try to talk   try to talk,
        just say something.
I can't, but I manage a smile.
Then, out of long silence,
    Hey, he says, *I want you to know*
    I was so glad
    when Malia called me on the ship,
    told me that she has a friend.
    And the son of the great Jacob Hirsch?
I smile, what does he mean, "the great"?
    Oh, and I am so sorry
    about the singing.
In my head I say, "Sorry?"
but nothing comes out.

Almost as if he heard
my thought he answers:
    Too much stress.
    It might cause more reactions.
    Anyway, he smiles,
    it is very nice to meet you at last.
    Go on, she's inside.

Change

Malia sits on her bed,
Blankie wrapped
around her head.
I sit in her desk chair.
Are you in there? I say.
>*It's all so stupid*, she says.
>*All of it.*
>*My father says I can't sing,*
>*that I need to put all my energy*
>*into getting well*
>*so I can go back to school.*

I try to think of what to say.
>*I don't care if they make fun of me.*
>*This is what I want to do most, Etan!*
>*I want to sing. Not be hidden away.*
Can't you talk to him? I ask.
Malia peeks out at me.
>*You don't know my father.*
>*He is a navy doctor.*
>*What he says goes.*

She rubs her arm.
It's a little redder than before,
but still clear.
>*I feel great, Etan.*
>*I think the clay*
>*is in my skin.*
>*It tingles.*
>*I feel like I can float,*
>*but he doesn't see it.*
>*He only sees*
>*"progress,"   but ...*

She gets up,
tiptoes like a cartoon character
toward her door and closes it.
I am going to do it anyway.

The Plan

Both my parents work Tuesday;
come get me.
I'll be ready.

What? I mean, *we shouldn't.*
My legs feel weak.
I can't imagine doing this,
but Malia seems so sure.
But won't Lola be here?
It will be fine, she says. *They won't know.*
We can tell Lola we are going to the forest.
For that long?
Etan. It would be so easy for me to not do it,
but I have been stuck at home for so long.
I'm NOT the creature!
I feel different,
I want to try!

I look for words.
I want to tell her I can't do it.
That I don't want to scare her parents,
or my grandfather,
but instead, something comes over me
like a strange chance,
an ancient bravery,
so I say, *Okay.*
Yes! She jumps on her bed,
her hands in fists.
I will be ready at noon!
So we'll have plenty of time
to get there by 4.
But school?
Etan, you missed school before.
Just this one day, okay?

The Difficult Choice

Malia *should* sing, go to school,
and do anything else she wants to,
and even though I like our plan,
I don't like that it's a secret—
doing something we shouldn't.
I feel the weight of this in every pedal,
like my tires spinning in the mud.

One difficult choice
to make, and suddenly
everything works its way in,
changes how everything looks.
      I should be at synagogue,
      studying, getting ready,
      but since my mom had to go
      everyone lets me do
      whatever I want to do
           and they leave me alone about it.
I know they want me to learn
to make my own decisions,
      but I don't want them
           to leave me alone.

The Meeting

Even with all these worries
swirling in my head,
I coast down into the town.
Around Main Street,
people are already everywhere.
I see my grandfather
through the shop window,
already back from synagogue,
a pile of books on his workbench,
but he's not alone. My father is there
in his Will Clark jersey and Giants hat,
his hands folded,
shoulders hunched,
like he always tells
me NOT to do.

I wait outside.
They are arguing.
My father moves
around the workbench,
his voice loud, muffled
through the window.
My grandfather
stands at his full height.
Most of the time he's
soft, bent over.
I forget
just how big
he actually is.

Handshake

My grandfather puts his hand out.

At school,
last time Martin
got in my face,
he called me a wimp,
told me I couldn't
play baseball anyway.
When the teacher heard it,
she made us talk about it.
I didn't really talk,
but I nodded a lot.
At the end,
she made us stand up,
face each other,
and shake hands
even though we didn't want to.
I wanted to believe
that would solve everything.

But this has to be different
because nobody is making them do it.

My grandfather steps forward
and puts out his hand
and my father puts out his,
but when he does,
my grandfather reaches in
with sudden strength
and pulls him in tight.
Maybe this is what a handshake
is supposed to be like,
because they look happy,
like they haven't been
for a long time.

Game 1

People decide to watch the game
near the center of Main Street
in the small park across
from Dimitri's Candy Shop.
Mr. Dimitri and some of the others
have rolled out his big TV,
one extension cord after the other
all the way across the street
where families lie on blankets
and sit in camping chairs.
Kids play baseball on the grass.
Jordan is there
with Martin and his older brother
and all the boys.
      I avoid them.

I bring Buddy to distract me,
his tail wagging against my leg,
everything a new smell,
something to investigate.
Smell of hot dogs
and grilling buns,
grass-stained jeans
and leather baseball mitts,
then woodsmoke from
a fireplace as the sun goes down,
and the dull glow
of the TV, the sound
turned so high
      that the speakers hum.

I haven't told my dad
about the talent show,
        the thought of it
            hovering like a giant bee
                buzzing in my mind.
I'll tell him today
before the game is over.

But by the fourth inning,
the A's have scored five runs,
and Giants fans get quiet.

Inning by inning
the outs come quick,
and by the seventh, most people
have already gone home.

Baseball Talk

More than playing baseball,
grown-ups like to *talk* about baseball.
That Rickey Henderson is hard to stop,
my grandfather says.
He is, my dad argues, *but those homers,*
what will happen tomorrow?
It feels good hearing them
talk like this.
I pick up Buddy.
He licks my face,
while my father and grandfather
go on like this
all the way back home.

Pre-Game 2

At the park, everything looks the same
except for one thing.
My grandfather sits on a camping chair
beneath a giant umbrella
away from everyone else,
talking to a family,
but not just any family.
      I see something
          I can't believe—
it's the Agbayanis!
When they see us
they all stand,
and there are so many
strange *hellos* and *nice to meet yous*.
Lola smiles at me,
and next to her is Malia,
wrapped in a scarf, sunglasses,
and a wide straw hat,
her lips frozen into a frown.
This is the first time
I've seen her
away from her house.
She doesn't move,
so I sit down next to her.
I pull out the notebook,
start flipping through doodles.
Look at this one, I say.
It's the golem.
      Well, can you make it come to life right now?

I look where's she's looking, and I see Martin and the other boys
staring at us in between their baseball game.
     I can't blame them, she says.
     I mean, look at me?
     Wrapped up like a mummy.
And it's then I notice
that people everywhere
are talking and eating all together,
     but no one
          is talking to the Agbayanis
               except for us.
I go over to Malia
with my mitt and baseball.
Want to play catch?
Malia looks at me,
a smile across her face,
she jumps up.

The mitt dangles from her hand,
then suddenly she launches the ball at me
with incredible strength.
I let it fly past me
since I don't have a mitt.
It soars, then bounces
all the way into the field,
right past Martin
to where Jordan is standing.

But before I can pick up the ball,
Martin puts his foot on it,
staring at it and then me,
then he lifts his arm
like he's throwing a fastball.

But I don't move,
     not an inch.
He laughs.
     Is the creature your girlfriend now?
I hold out my hand
for him to give me the ball.
     No way! I'm not touching this thing after she did.
He moves his foot off the ball.
Jordan walks over,
     picks the ball up from the ground,
                         puts it in my hand.

Game 2

My grandfather and Mr. Cohen
stop talking long enough
to see when Candy Maldonado
launches the ball from right field
and gets Dave Parker out at second.
But the umpire calls him safe,
and the park goes crazy!
Grown-ups use words
kids aren't allowed to hear.
Mr. Dimitri slams the cover
of his grill, and charcoal bits
fly into the air!
Malia whispers, *Was that a bad call?*
     And then   on almost   the very next play,
          Terry Steinbach hits a home run.
       Three A's score.
          The A's fans let it out,
             swinging green flags,
               chanting out names.
    But my father starts to slowly clap,
looking around, trying to create hope.
It's okay. It's okay. Wait till Tuesday. Game 3.
    We get to see what they're made of!

Departing

People peel away from the park
and before Malia goes,
she carefully rewraps her scarf,
whispers in my ear,
See you Tuesday, Etan. Okay?
    Don't forget our plan.

What Are We Made Of?

It's already dark
when we finally get home;
the apartment seems
emptier than ever.
My father throws our stuff
on the kitchen counter,
sits in the middle of the sofa
staring at the TV
even though it's off.
He pats the cushion next to him.
I sit down, and he puts his arm around me.
I lean my head on his shoulder.
> *Well, I guess on Tuesday*
> *we'll see what the Giants are made of.*
The words swirl around in my mind.
Everyone says that. What does it mean? I ask.
> *What they are made of?*
He thinks for a while,
tapping my shoulder lightly.
> *You know*, he says slowly, *like what's inside you, I guess?*
> *Girls are sugar, spice, and all the rest . . .*
I don't say anything. It can't just be that.
> *I guess that's not it.*
> *I guess it's about who you are.*
> *What you have been through,*
> *how you handle things*
> *when things get tough.*
> *Like the Giants are having a tough series,*
> *so we have to see if they can pull off a win.*
What if they don't win?
> *Well, I guess it's not always about winning.*
> *Sometimes it's just about believing in yourself.*

And then he leans in.
>*Being brave*
>>*even if it seems*
>>>*like you don't have any chance*
>>>*of winning.*

I look at him, and he continues.

Like your grandpa, and Mrs. Li,
and everyone else,
leaving everything they knew,
all of who they were,
through all those countries,
and then taking a ship
while the world was falling to pieces
just to land on Angel Island—
starting a whole new life
>*in a strange place.*

He hugs me a little tighter.
I think about the past few weeks
and the idea of what we are made of,
and I can't help but think
how tough Malia is,
that she must be made
of the strongest stuff.
And then the words just come out.
Malia had to leave school
and kids call her that stupid name,
but they just don't know
how hard it is for her.
He looks up.
>*That's right.*

We sit there for a while.

And finally
I let my last
tired thought
come out.

Like Mom, too?

    Yeah.
        He breathes, deeply.   *Just like Mom.*

October 16

At school
there are a few A's fans
in their jerseys talking loud,
but mostly, everyone is quiet.
At lunch, I sit near the field.
I sketch the Golden Gate.
The long belly of the bridge
stretches from one tower to the other,
and just beyond is where my mom is.
> *Etan!*
It's Jordan, he's holding a mitt.
> *Etan, we need someone to play left.*
Jeremy had to go home 'cause his stomach hurts.
Martin holds the ball, stares at me.
I start to shake my head no,
but then something happens.
Maybe it's the sound of his voice,
or all that's been happening,
I think, what *am* I made of?
I stand up,
putt on the mitt,
slowly walk out to left field.
Martin growls at me,
Don't mess it up.
> The field is grass forever
> > and foggy skies
> > > and too many people.
Martin pitches,
> and then
> > in slow motion,
Josh hits the ball
> so hard it goes invisible,
> > until the moment

I see it coming right for me,
　　already on its way down.
　　　　I hold out my mitt,
　　　　　　feel the eyes of everyone
　　　　on my every move.
　　　　　　This is the very last thing
　　　　　　　　I wanted to happen.
And then, all at once, I feel
the sudden, perfect weight
of the ball, square in the webbing
of the leather mitt.
　　　　I smile
　　　　　　because I caught it!
But it doesn't matter
　　　　because by then the earth
　　　　　　is already shaking.

The tremor doesn't last long,
but enough for everyone to line up
like our drills teach us.
This isn't the first tremor
　　to hit us this week,
　　　　but
　　　　　　it will be the last.

The Agbayanis

At the shop,
my grandfather is bending over,
picking up a few screws that jumped
out of their containers during the tremor.
I tell him about my catch,
he coughs a little, punches me in the arm.
>*Are you going to your friend's today?*
>*The last day before the show?*
Not today. I should be there
when Dad gets home.
I hope he's not mad
that I'm not going to the game.
>*You need to tell him. He will understand.*
>*And besides, we will ALL be there.*
All of you? I ask.
>*We would not miss it.*
I think about our plan,
sneaking away to sing.
>I never thought about this,
>>that everyone might come;
>>>her parents will find out for sure!
>>>Why did we think we could keep it a secret?
>>>*Grandpa, you can't invite Malia's parents.*
>>>*She'll be in trouble!*
Etan, it's okay, the Agbayanis are part of us.

The Truth

I can't sleep because
Game 3,
     the talent show,
the plan,
      my mom,
and everything swirling.

I dream about
Buddy barking wildly
and biting my pants,
trying to tell me something.
Then, all of a sudden, I am
slipping into the muck
of the pool,
the clay pulling me
deep down inside it,
the trees reaching
long wooden arms,
trying to pull me out.

My father wakes me up,
makes me eggs and toast.
Today's the day, he says. *Go Giants!*
But I know that I need to tell him
that I am going to the talent show.
Then the phone rings.
It's my mom,
      and she wants to talk to me.

When you don't talk a lot
I think your ears get stronger.
So now, sometimes,
I feel I can hear the meaning of words,
the shape of their sound.
  My mom's words are light,
   silver clouds in a blue sky.
She tells me that she's coming home soon.   Coming home.
   Home:
   I smell the wood and metal
   of my grandfather's shop,
   feel the coolness
   of the Sitting Stones
   beneath the redwoods,
   smell the skin lotion
   Malia wears,
   like vanilla and sunlight.
    But the shape of the word
   changes when my mom says it,
   like ice cream melting on the cone,
   or the soft voice
    before going to sleep,
    reminding me
    that I am made
    of just the right stuff.

I whisper everything to her
about Malia and the talent show
and the tickets to the game.
    What do I do, Mom?
   She's quiet
    for so long
     that I wonder
if she's really okay.

Tell your father, she says.
Tell him I said you could go,
that you should go,
that I promised you
that he would understand.
I love you, Etan.
          I will see you soon.

I walk over to the couch,
hand him his coffee.
Dad, I need to tell you something.
          And I tell him everything all at once—
          about the talent show
          and sorry for not telling him sooner
          and about what Mom said.
He listens for a long time,
          stands up,
                    walks around the couch once,
goes into the bathroom,
                    closes the door.
When he finally comes out,
          he sits down silently,
                    puts his arm around me.

          I understand.
He lets out a long breath.
I'll take Mike to the game
straight from work;
we have a job near the city.
I'll probably be home late,
who knows, maybe
you'll see me on TV?

I can't tell if he's upset
or really okay,
or maybe just surprised
by Mom's words.
He gets his keys,
and I wheel out my bike.
Tell Malia "Break a leg!"
I will see you guys late tonight.
We can celebrate the Giants
because tonight they are going to win!

The Day of Days

On the boldest day
of my entire life,
I feel the least brave.
I ride my bike to school.
11:45: Lunch bell rings.
11:49: I unlock my bike,
and ride,
    standing up,
        as fast as I can,
            all the way
                to Forest Road.
12:27: On the very last stretch
of road, before the dragon mailbox,
I try to listen
    to the trees,
        but they are silent and still.

12:31: Arrival

I hide my bike outside the driveway,
peer through the bushes;
              no one's outside.
I creep around the back of the house,
sweating from the bike ride.

Malia is there
in her window.
She sees me,
dramatically points down
to the front door,
which opens suddenly.

Lola is standing there.
     Hello, Etan?
In my mind
I form the best lying sentence
about how school let out early,
but nothing comes out.

Malia blunders down the stairs.
Hi, Etan! Lola, we're going for a bike ride,
then down to the creek
for the afternoon. Love you!
She kisses her on the cheek,
her overstuffed backpack
like a turtle shell, sunglasses on,
scarf around her whole head.
Before Lola says anything,
we are out the door,
Malia holding my arm.
Then we go to her garage,
where her purple Huffy
with ribbons on the handlebars
leans against the side.

Nervous

Are you nervous? I say.
Malia scratches her arms through her shirt,
opens a cough drop.
>   *Yes! Duh!*
Do you want to practice?
>   *Yes! But we need to take the long way*
>   *down to our place*
>   *so Lola doesn't see us*
>   *going through the yard.*

We get our bikes,
walk the long way
through paths I haven't seen before.
The October forest is warmer than I've ever felt,
like the smell of my grandfather's shop
in the morning before the air comes in.

Malia stops.
>   *I can't hear the trees, Etan.*
>   *Something is happening.*

I stop,   look around,
Try to listen, too.

The stones wait for us
near the pool,
where the water
is a sheet of glass,
a mirror, perfectly flat.

We sit on the stones,
face each other,
staring quietly
in a long and nervous silence.

I think of my grandfather.
What would he say?
Okay, Malia, are you ready?
Show me what you're made of.
Slowly she takes off her sunglasses,
her eyes wrinkle together.
      What? Wait, what are you talking about?
      She looks confused.
I look down,
my legs nervously shaking.
Never mind, I say. *So are you ready?*
      No! she shouts. *How could I ever be?*
We try to stop shaking,
and eventually
she breathes,
    listens,
        her body shifts,
and in the stillness
    of the strange afternoon air
        her voice fills the forest.

Maybe, I think,
the trees are quiet
because today
    they are listening
        to her.

Granola Bars

She opens her backpack,
pulls out a box of apple fruit granola bars.
Here, she says, *eat, we have to keep our strength up.*
The bars crumble in our hands.
> *Do you think a lot of people will be there?*
I imagine all the people filling the community center.
I think about
the *Calypso,*
that we're all connected
like a giant family,
that so many people
will be there tonight,
> everyone except her parents,
> who don't even know,
> but they will definitely find out.

But Malia is standing now,
her scarf unwrapped,
and even though the swelling in her eye
is not that different,
the redness of her skin
still a slight shine in places,
she seems so much freer.

She spins near the pool
and her body moves in the windless air.

> *I think I am ready, Etan! Nervous, but ready!*
> *I feel like all of our days here*
> *have really, you know, put me together.*
> *I feel like myself inside my own skin,*
> *like I could handle anything.*

The Last Lunch

We pack everything
and get ready for our journey,
when we hear something
moving down the path—
    the sound of shuffling shoes
        the sudden and bright flowery dress.
            Lola?
She comes to the stones,
holds out a platter
where mangoes are cut into cubes.
    So lovely here, she says.
    Like home maybe.
We eat mangoes,
unsure of what to do next.

    So quiet today?
She looks at me.
Malia laughs, pushes my shoulder.
He's always quiet.
Then Lola stares straight at us,
her face serious, voice low.
    But you won't be quiet later, will you?
        When it's time to siiiiing?
Malia coughs up a mango,
spits it into her hand.
LOLA! But, how . . .
I feel a wave of fear,
a wave of relief.
Lola smiles,
rests her hand on Malia's head.

It's okay, anak.
Grown-ups know everything.
You are safe with me.
Sing with all of your heart.
Now, you better get going!

We ride fast down Forest Road.
How did she know? Malia asks.
I don't know, I say.
But it feels good,
and every pedal
feels better,
    like riding closer
        to exactly where we are supposed to go.

Part 6

The Community Center

Malia isn't the best bike rider.
She's wobbly, and she knows it.
    What?!
She looks at me, almost crashing,
but we make it through town,
past the park where everyone
is gathering again
for the third game of the Series.

We reach the community center right at three.
The Covenanteers are there,
hats in full bloom,
welcoming all the talent,
holding big bowls of apples,
Fruit Roll-Ups, and water cups.

We pass by the little gym,
full of chairs lined in perfect rows
all the way to the stage.

In the rec room,
kids and parents are everywhere.
    Tiny ballerinas spin
    on the slippery floor.
    One boy holds up a pickle
    while his little dog
    leaps in the air,
    its jaws snapping.
And then,
I see Jordan there, holding a guitar,
trying to play through chords.

When he sees us,
he smiles, waves.
I wave back.
        Hi, Malia, he says. *You feeling better?*
Malia, her head scarf-wrapped,
sunglasses tight, her Cyndi Lauper
cassette tape wrapped tightly
inside Blankie,
smiles wide. *Hi . . . Jordan.*
He stops playing and looks up.
        Hey, you guys going
        to the park with everyone after this?
        First pitch at 5:35?
        It's Candlestick this time.
        I bet they are going to wreck the A's.

We find our own corner of the rec room.
Malia lays out Blankie
like we're at a picnic.
We sit, open the program.
It says she's fourteenth, just after Molly,
who's playing piano,
and before William,
who is doing a monologue
from Shakespeare.

She curls her knees into her arms,
hugs them tightly,
rocks back and forth
to the timing of the music,
the lyrics forming on her lips.

Right Before:

Malia puts her hand on my foot.
>*I don't feel like the creature any more.*

Because you never were! I say.
>*Remember you asked me*
>*what I am made of?*

I feel my face redden.
>*It was a good question, Etan.*
>*I just want to say thanks.*
>*I think part of me feels*
>*like it's made of clay,*
>*the old clay and the new clay from the river,*
>*and my Lola's adobo,*
>*and my grandfather's dragon mailbox,*
>*and your drawings.*
>*All of it all together.*

Malia can say everything
on her mind all at once.

Are you ready? I say.

>She looks around the room.
>*Almost,* she says.

She unwraps the scarf
from around her head,
takes off her glasses,
her swollen eye partially closed,
that side of her face,
a little red from the eczema.
She breathes deeply.
>*When we go in, will you hold Blankie?*

3:52

While the rec room
takes deep breaths
with everyone getting ready to perform,
I peek out the door and into the gym
to see if anyone is actually here yet.

It's full.

Parents, grandparents, teachers,
everyone dressed in Giants jerseys
and hats, the Covenanteers
handing out cookies
and Dixie cups of Crystal Light.
I walk over to get a cup for Malia,
and then, near the front,
already seated,   I see them:
        my grandfather,   Mrs. Li,   Mr. Cohen,
and more empty seats.

3:58

Malia gulps down the punch,
      throws the cup at me,
                    laughs.
I need to tell you.
      Tell me what?
I mean, it's no big deal.
      What!! she demands.
Well, just that
my grandfather,
and Mrs. Li, Mr. Cohen,
and maybe some others, well, you should know
that they are   here.
Her eyes widen
      and she coughs.
      But my parents. They'll tell my parents . . .
Don't you think they were going to find out anyway?
      Malia picks up the cup,
      throws it at me again.
We hear the loud screech
of a microphone,
      a muffled voice,
            the show is starting.

4:08

The host looks over at us.
All right, Jordan,
you are starting us off.
Jordan grabs his guitar like a rock star,
walks toward the stage.
Tammy Stinton, you are next!
Tammy skips toward the stage
with a recorder in her hand.

4:14

We can't really see onto the stage
but we hear guitar chords
and the occasional clapping,
the voice of the emcee,
and finally Jordan
makes his way back in,
holding his guitar in one hand.
He packs up his stuff.
See you guys later at the park?

4:27

Malia paces   ,
and I go out to the tables
to get her another cup of punch
and that's when I see it.
All the way by the stage,
the seats that were empty before
are filled.
         Mr. and Mrs. Agbayani!
Lola must have told them!
But I don't see her.
I bring the punch to Malia,
         and I say
                  absolutely nothing.

4:36

When the little ballerina
slips on stage,
her parents
pick her up,
help her finish,
to a standing ovation.

4:45

Molly waits nervously,
steps onto the stage,
and that means
Malia is next.
She gets up,
crumples Blankie into a ball,
and puts it in my arms.
   Don't lose Blankie!
She looks at her cassette
to make sure it's wound to the right place,
then hands her cassette to the Covenanteer,
who takes it to the theater tech.
We look at each other,
and I think something
like a prayer in mind.

Molly plays "The Entertainer,"
and when she finishes,
she plays the whole thing again.
Malia stands up on her toes
and back down
   and up again.
William stands
way too close to her,
since he's next,
the sleeves of his shirt way too long,
a Shakespeare wig fixed to his head
leaning slightly to the left.
My heart feels tight
from the pressure of breathing.

I want to be on the Sitting Stones
near the pool,
both of us
listening to the trees.
When I look at her,
she's holding one hand
over her swollen eye.
        You can do it! I whisper.

4:52

Please welcome Malia Agbayani!
I wait without breath until
I hear the applause.

Singing

When Malia sings,
it's like stones dropping into a deep pool
or skipping across the surface,
      but more than that;
      her voice has so much light,
      a voice that understands
      the language of the trees,
      the language of her family,
      and even me who has trouble
      saying anything at all.
I listen to the words fill the gym,
amazed at the beautiful quiet
of "Time After Time,"
and I feel like she's singing the song to me.
Then I remember
her parents sitting in the front row,
and I wonder
if a mountain of trouble
is about to fall
      on our heads.

4:58

Applause.
Loud, like at a baseball game.
I peek around the corner.
Malia stands on stage
and everyone is cheering,
she's smiling,
        she can't stop.
My grandfather and Mrs. Li
wipe tears away.
Her parents are watery-eyed, too.
The applause lasts for a whole minute.

5:01

Malia walks backward
off the stage waving, smiling,
eyes bright,
        shining,
                even as she bumps
into William
holding onto his wig
for dear life.

5:03

Malia hugs me tight.
Did you hear it!
And I can tell
she's crying
into my shoulder,
then she pulls back
and launches her fist
into the same shoulder.

> *My parents are out there!*
> > *Did you know? Did you?*

I don't know what to say.
How can someone be so happy
and so angry all at the same time.
She punches my shoulder again.
> *Tell me, Etan!*

5:04

Somewhere
    deep inside
        the earth lets go.

Fifteen Seconds

I fall.
The ground is not the ground.
We fall
against the wall of the rec room,
the windows shatter,
the sound of applause
turns to shouting,
hundreds of grown-up voices
swirling together at once
into a trumpet of confusion.
      The ceiling explodes,
          plaster and dust
              rain like water
                    on our heads,
we are covered in white.
The ground is shaking
       for fifteen seconds;
          it won't stop.
We try to get up,
but it's moving too fast,
and the air is made of sounds
from everything we can't see.

Words,   skin,   clay,
nothing matters
except trying to find
something solid to hold on to.

We crawl
        to the snack table
                and get underneath,
dragging
        everyone we see
                until we are bodies
overflowing
        in a too-small box.
Some grown-ups
come in through the wings,
falling into broken plaster,
the ground throwing them
every which way.
Their arms reaching for us.
We hold on to each other
        until the earth
exhales
        a low rumble,
until everything
        is finally still.

5:06

The shouting
starts.
Malia's skin
is white with plaster dust,
her face like a ghost.
Grown-ups
pour into the room,
     scoop up kids,
          and disappear.

     Etan, we need to get outside.
Malia pulls me up
and we step over
what was,
     just a few seconds before,
          a table with juice and cookies.
We step between twisted light fixtures
          and broken glass.

5:07

Near the door
is the little ballerina,
the top of her tutu ripped,
standing in the middle of window glass,
her thumb in her mouth,
her hand bleeding a little.

Malia lifts her up,
        looks around,
then reaches for my hand
        and pulls Blankie
                from my still-clenched fist.

She shakes it out
        and wraps the ballerina
                in a messy cocoon.

5:07

There are people running
in all directions,
some trying to get out,
some trying to get in,
all of them yelling,
and the sounds of sirens in the distance.
Outside, the light is pale.
Somewhere on Main Street
a fire is burning.
We breathe,
something like clean air.
Malia looks around,
       carrying the little girl,
          her head pressed against
             her shoulder.

5:08

A silver-haired woman
sobs so much
she can't talk.
She wobbles over to us,
reaches out,
takes the girl in her arms.

We look
     for my grandfather,
          for her parents.
   I think of my mom,
        so far away,
             and my dad.
Maybe where he is
     it wasn't so bad.

5:09

Lines of fire trucks
peel down the street,
create a wall of spinning lights,
    red metal against the sky.

No power.

We push against families making their way outside,
toward the front of the rec center.
    Every light fell from the ceiling,
    fluorescent bulb glass
    and metal wires webbed
    across turned over chairs.

Momma! Malia screams.
        I try to yell, but nothing comes,
                and then I see my grandfather.
He's still in his chair.
Mr. Agbayani is kneeling next to him.
        Just breathe, Jacob, breathe.
But he's coughing,
like all the dust in the air
went straight down his throat.

Mrs. Agbayani is talking
to a mother and daughter;
Mrs. Li walks a woman by the arm.
We rush to the front.
Mr. Agbayani throws his arms around
his daughter, looks her in the eye.
Can you get water?   She runs off.

Etan . . . my grandfather coughs. *You're all right*, he says.
Etan, he grabs my wrist,
squeezes with all his strength,
and I feel his hand closing
around my arm
like he might never let go.

5:11

He looks me in the eye
and smiles, coughs.
Etan, it's all right.
And then,
every word that's hidden away
turns into one giant yell.
  Grandpa!
    Grandpa.
He coughs and coughs.
Malia hands a cup of water
to her dad, and he pours
it down Grandpa's throat.
The water gurgles
out, over his chin.

Malia looks at me.
Etan . . .
   She reaches into her pocket,
       pulls out her Tic Tac container,
           pops open the top.
The clay inside
smells like the forest
and the pool,
like my grandfather's shop
and the ancient box.
She scoops it out with her finger.
What do we pray?
And then I think of Yom Kippur,
that THIS CAN'T BE GRANDPA'S TIME.

She reaches for his neck.
Malia, what is that?
Mr. Agbayani puts his hand out,
    but she stops it.
          It's okay, Poppa. It's okay.
Malia spreads the clay
on his throat
while he coughs.
Water tries to make
its way down and back up again.
She smears the clay,
and I pray near his ear
    until
        at last
            the coughing stops.

5:12

BOOM,
> *BOOM,*
BOOM!
> In low rumbles,
something is exploding
near and far away.

5:12

Grandpa breathes,
opens his eyes,
but they circle
in his head,
> a man
>> not himself,
>>> looking
through time and space,
> trying to find where he is,

finally settling on Mrs. Li
and Mr. Agbayani, and me.

We get to our feet,
shuffle through broken
tables, plaster bits,
shattered glass,
purses, cameras
smashed in pieces.

5:14

On Main Street
     fires burn
          in different buildings.
Everything is broken.
We shuffle through streets
holding each other up,
block by block,
Mr. Cohen's bakery,
Mrs. Li's market,
people wandering
in all directions.

5:15

Malia walks
with her head down,
leaning on her mother's shoulder,
scratching her arm.
I want to pull her hand away.

5:16

Along Main Street
people sit in their cars,
radios on,
there are voices
in the air
with street names and instructions:
Bay Bridge   Broken
     Jefferson Street Marina   On Fire

The Gape

In front of the bakery,
the crack in the earth
is a gaping mouth.
The earth has opened
and the stones
that make the street
have fallen in,
straight down into some
unknown place.
The crack stretches
to the alley
where the names
of the people
from the *Calypso*
are listed.
I wonder
if they've fallen in, too.

5:18

The world is not itself.
It feels held together
by a huddle of people.

Somewhere out there is my mother;
somewhere out there is my father.

5:19

Did you hear?
The whole stadium
was shaking
like a bomb went off.
Mr. Dimitri
is walking from the park
holding baskets of rock candy
and lollipops, handing them out.
The Bay Bridge, too—collapsed!
Mrs. Agbayani gasps.
        The whole thing?
Don't know, he says.
My grandfather coughs.

5 . . .

We open the shop.
Screws and metal pieces
are scattered across the floor,
every cup is spilled.
The window is unbroken
but the trophies and medals
are piled on the floor,
shelves turned over,
broken, flat.
      I see the treasure box
          perfectly together
              like an island
                    in a rough sea.
The Agbayanis help my grandfather
sit in his big chair near the back.
He grabs Mrs. Li's hand.
      Your store?
Then so many things happen
all at the same time.
Mrs. Li goes outside,
looks at her store,
where the wood shelves
full of fruit have given way
and apples fill the street.

Mr. Agbayani tries the phone,
but the lines are all busy.
Malia folds her arms around her body.
　　　I'm sorry about Blankie, I say.
She looks at me with something like a smile.
Our bikes! she says. *And your notebook?*
I picture everything buried
beneath a fallen ceiling.
I wish I had my green stone.

We feel for the ghosts of things
that once made us feel safe.

Darkness

Mrs. Agbayani sets up candles around the shop,
gives us all glasses of water.
We'll know more soon, she says.
I picture my mother
at the hospital,
my father at the stadium
or in his truck,
trying to find his way
to us.
He'll be here.
I hope.

Home

For the first time
I think of our apartment.
Is the building still standing?
Is everything on the floor?

Then, quietly,
people wander into the shop,
carrying food and other things,
setting them on the workbench
or near the window.
Asking if they can rest here.
It is one of the oldest stores in town.
Maybe they feel safe here, with us.
Soon there are families
sitting together in picnics,
like the park in the summer.
My grandfather calls me over,
pointing to everyone.
    Like Shabbos, right?

Mr. Dimitri tunes his radio in,
        7.0 on the Richter scale,
and we know that's a high number.

Buddy

In the doorway
we see the sniffing nose,
the furry little body.
Isn't that—
    I look—
        Buddy?
His tongue out,
       he jumps
           into Malia's lap.
And then I remember. *Grandpa!*
Mrs. Hershkowitz!
He looks at me,
puts his heavy hand on my shoulder.
     You have to check, Etan,
     can you do that?
Mrs. Agbayani and Malia
agree to come,
and the three of us
and Buddy go out into the street.

Mrs. Hershkowitz

On our way
we see a group of boys—
Jordan holding his broken guitar,
and Martin, and his brother.
I look at Malia,
but she doesn't care.
Mrs. Agbayani stops.
Are you boys okay? Can you help us?
    They nod,
            and we rush to the building.

The glass doors
at the front of our building
are shattered into pieces.
I see her window open,
the basket on the street below it.
We step carefully over the glass,
flashlights beam
through dark hallways,
and the cluster of us
walk stair by stair
slowly, along creaking wood.
Buddy stands at her door
at the end of the hall,
where light fixtures have fallen,
broken onto the carpet.
He barks, sniffs
at the five-inch crack in the door.
I push on the door
but it's stuck.
Malia pushes next to me,
still stuck.
    Mrs. Herskowitz? I call out, nothing.

Malia presses her face against the door.
There's something blocking it.
Then Martin steps right between us,
with his brother and Jordan.
They pile on the door and push it slowly open.
Buddy leaps in,
darts between fallen
          bookcases,
the same one that fell before,
its books spread out everywhere,
and Mrs. Hershkowitz
close to the window,
a broken teacup near her hand.

I kneel by Mrs. Hershkowitz.
Mrs. Agbayani presses a wet rag
against her forehead,
snaps her fingers
in front of her eyes,
and slowly she wakes up.
Buddy licks her face.
The boys move bookcases
out of the way.
Malia and Jordan
stack books against the walls.
Then, like the world getting up,
the sudden whir
of the refrigerator going on,
the static of the TV, the blink and shine of the lights
like we're waking up from some strange dream.

The Things That Happen Next

When Mrs. Hershkowitz
is all set in her chair
and she's kissed us all on the cheek,
and the neighbors give her a glass of water,
with Buddy happily coiled at her feet,
we head downstairs.
By now I can't stop thinking about
my parents, but every phone line is busy.
When we get outside,
Jordan comes over,
and then,
     all of a sudden,
          he wraps an arm around me.
      Sorry about everything, Etan.
The boys start to head up the street
but just before, Martin looks over
like he might say sorry, or something else,
but he just looks at me,
then Malia.
       See you at school sometime I guess?
       I mean when you come back.
         Yep! she says,
and the thought of school
suddenly seems
like the very place we want to be.

The Drive

Mr. Agbayani drives up,
headlights beaming
on one million flecks
of lingering dust
thrown up by the earth.

Your grandfather is with Mrs. Li.
Do you want to come with us?
We need to check on Lola, and the house.

Malia grabs my hand,
    pulls me in,
        and we speed up Forest Road,
            not knowing what we will find.

Return to Forest Road

I gaze through windows
at flickering lights,
and fires dying down
in the twilight sky.
It feels safe, warm
inside the car,
and Malia looks over at me,
      whispers, *Are you okay, Etan?*
I am okay,
like something inside me,
some different strength
I didn't know I had
is at work.
Yes, I say.
      Good, because I am NOT okay.
      I mean, I finally sing
      and then the earthquake happens?
Silence, and then we smile.
Her parents, though,
are not smiling.
Her mom is crying,
she turns.
      Malia. And then so many words in Tagalog.
            Yes, Momma.
But she can't seem to say anything,
      her face turned down,
      her father looking forward at the road,
      until I see his shoulders soften.
      Malia, he says, his words tight,
          your singing was beautiful.

Mailbox

The lights in the neighborhood
are slowly turning on.
People are outside their homes.
There are trees fallen in the road,
mailboxes turned over. Our headlights shine
on the eyes of the dragon,
still standing with its slippery tongue out,
but as we pull in we see something
we can't believe.
>   The front porch is broken,
>   smashed into the ground.
>   Shoes sprinkle through
>   broken boards.

Lola

Mrs. Agbayani races from the car
screaming, *LOLA*!
And we follow, *LOLA!*
I look up at Malia's window
where the glass is broken,
wood sliding off in all directions.
We run to the back door
near the field,
the trees, the path
darkening beneath the clear sky.

Lola is there
sitting in an Adirondack chair
in the backyard,
a small candle burning
on a table next to her,
the phone pulled all the way
out from the living room.
In her lap, an old, gray photo album.
        Of course, Mr. Agbayani grunts.
They run to hug Lola,
who quickly stands,
and then disappears inside with them.
But when she sees me,
she waves me over, too.

We roll a small TV out
from the living room
onto the back porch.
We move the antenna around,
find channel 7,
wavy-lined, staticky breaking news,
straight from Candlestick Park.

Peter Wilson, the reporter,
tries to describe what happened.
He holds his earpiece tight.
     We're hearing that the quake
     was centered in South Bay
     near the Santa Cruz Mountains.
That's us, Mrs. Agbayani gasps.

We watch for a long time,
baseball fans huddled
behind the reporter.
I look for my dad.
Our eyes follow every scene.
Reporters argue if the game will go on—
if it should go on.
Fires burn in San Francisco.
     Fire trucks rolling,
         hydrants bursting water,
              roads everywhere
                 cracked and broken,
and then we see it,
     the Bay Bridge.
         The two layers
             intersect,
                a piece of the top, split,
            broken, falling down
              into itself,
                  cars trapped underneath.

Malia puts her hand on my shoulder.
Your father is okay, Etan,
I know he is.
The reporter tells us
that people have been asked
to leave Candlestick Park
to return home in an "orderly manner."

Malia walks to the edge of the field,
the path to the Sitting Stones
growing faint in the dying light.
She touches the tree.
I know she is listening.
  What's it saying, I ask her.
     She looks at me,
      slowly walks back,
whispers in my ear,
      Everything.

Getting Back

Mr. Agbayani decides
that the back half of the house
is safe for now,
and when everyone
is settled, he drives me
to the shop.
      Before I go,
Malia walks me to the car.
          Can you believe this day?
She tries to sound funny.
I laugh because, as always,
something about her makes
me feel like everything is actually okay.
      Everything we've done,
      all the arguments,
          the practices,
              itchiness,
                  silence,
                     worry,
      and even the ancient magic clay,
      all seems a little silly now
      with everything crumbled away,
      like suddenly none of it
      matters at all.
But it has to matter, doesn't it?
It has to mean something.

Malia grabs my hand.
Thank you, Etan,
for being part of my plan,
for sharing your secrets with me.
She points to her empty Tic Tac container.
It worked, didn't it?
I mean, it really, really worked.
I think to myself: I don't know how it worked,
but it seems like something did.
     And then she hugs me
             like she's my family.

Questions on the Drive

Mr. Agbayani can tell I feel nervous,
so he assures me that my father
must be fine.
He asks me lots of questions
about baseball,
kosher food,
earthquakes,
the *Calypso*,
being Jewish,
     about whether the plan
     was mine or hers,
and then, at last,
just as we pull through back roads
onto Main Street
he asks me,
his voice suddenly wobbly and quiet:
     When this all calms down,
     and things, you know,
     get put back together,
     what do you think?
          Will Malia be okay
               at school?
I'm so used to saying nothing,
used to searching for words
deep in my belly
or having them get stuck
in my throat,
that I'm surprised when they just appear.
     She's gonna be awesome,
     Mr. Agbayani.
     No one is like Malia.

Part

7

Find Him

My grandpa is at his workbench now.
Mr. Dimitri is there with Mr. Cohen and Mrs. Li,
and they are drinking out of metal cups
that my grandfather keeps
for the most special occasions.
A small TV with its rabbit ears up
plays next to them.

I have seen these people
together like this my whole life,
and it's a safe and steady thing.
My grandfather waves me over,
puts his arms around me,
my face burying into his chest.
     I'm so tired.
I hear the soft vibrations
   of their voices
     saying my name,
      holding me from every side,
  and for the first time
    all day,
     I let go.

Mrs. Li gives me a cup of hot chocolate.
I let the steam warm my face.

They talk and watch the TV;
news reports cut back and forth
with cartoon pictures of the Santa Cruz Mountains
and the San Andreas Fault like a dark river.
People pointing to broken glass,
and streets curved and out of order.

Candlestick Park over and over
and the reporter talking about
        "the game that didn't happen."
Each time they show it,
my grandfather holds me closer,
whispers in Hebrew
to me,   to himself.
I pull away from his chest,
look at him closely,
the clay smeared dry on this throat.
I'm okay, he says. *Your father, he'll be okay, too.*
I drink the hot chocolate
and rest there
        until their voices,
                strong voices I've heard
                        my whole life,
fold over me like a blanket,
and my eyes begin to close,
heavy with steaming chocolate
and thoughts of everything
that happened in a single day.
I feel myself
                falling
                        asleep.

Wake Up

I open my eyes because it feels
like I am falling
or the ground is shaking.
I grab onto the chair,
my grandfather's big brown chair.
I'm in it. There's a blanket on me.
The world is not shaking.

Light, sunlight
through the windows of the shop,
the smell of coffee, the low hum
of my grandfather's voice
and someone else's.
I rub my eyes.
  Did it really happen?
  What day is it?
  Then my body tightens
  and I remember everything.
  Plaster and glass and the ballerina
  and everything breaking apart
  and the image of the Bay Bridge.
  And I hide under the torn blue blanket,
  pull it tight around my head.

You're awake!

The muffled voice,
the hand on my shoulder
peeling back the blanket,
and I feel my whole body lift,
            swing in the air,
my body wrapped tightly
            around his
                    like I am five years old,
                            my head buried in his shoulder,
the smell of earth and wood dust,
            the smell of   my father.
            He's holding me
                        and I start crying
                                and I can't stop.

The Quake

Mr. Cohen smiles at me
while I eat the biggest jelly donut
he's ever baked, and we listen
to my father tell the story.
>   *It was a wild party,*
>   *the game was about to start.*
>   *We watched the recap*
>   *of Jose Canseco crossing the plate,*
>   *the crowd making all the noises*
>   *and then the picture just started to crackle,*
>   *and there's Al Michaels,*
>   *he cuts in, says,*
>   *"You know what . . . I think we're having an earth—"*
>   *and everything went dark,*
>   *and it was like a giant steamroller*
>   *came out of right field*
>   *and rammed full speed into the 'Stick.*
>   *The upper deck shaking,*
>   *escalators blowing off their tracks,*
>   *everyone screaming, screaming, screaming . . .*

He pauses. Everyone is breathing loudly,
Mr. Cohen and my grandfather
like little kids at story time.
>   *But you know what?*
>   *Candlestick stood up to the quake.*

The strangest part,
people just walking on the grass
      inside the diamond,
         through the dugouts,
no more players or fans,
      no more A's or Giants,
         the green and the orange
            mixing all together,
    just everyone looking out for each other.
Me and my buddy carried
a man with a hurt leg
all the way across the field.

My grandfather hugs my father,
looks at me.
    Etan, I already told your father
    about our adventures here,
    but I think you two should talk.

Sorry

We walk outside into the sunlight.
People are everywhere,
cleaning streets,
talking together,
some stores open,
others closed.
        What would I be doing
        if I were in school right now?
But nobody is at school today.

I tell him about Malia,
and our plan,
and the singing.

He listens like a new man,
his arm around me,
tears coming from his eyes.
        Etan, he says, kneeling down,
            putting both hands
                on my shoulders.
        Sorry I wasn't here with you.

Surprise

When I finally got to the truck,
we didn't know where we could even drive.
No traffic lights,   no anything,   just chaos.
We didn't even know what roads were broken;
                if we could drive on them at all.

We'd heard that the upper deck of the Bay Bridge came down,
        like the world was ending.
I even thought of driving out to the old mining road,
                circling all the way around.
But you know what? I had to get where I was going,
                and it took me all night, but I made it.
I look at him.   Where? I ask.
        He squints at the sun.
To Langley Hospital,
                near Golden Gate Park,
                                to get your mom.

Our Building

The doorway to the apartment building
is hollowed out, the glass cleaned up,
the debris swept away.
Mrs. Hershkowitz leans out her window
as soon as she sees me.

> *ETAN! CAN YOU TAKE BUDDY TO THE PARK?*
> *HE'S GOTTA GO, BAD!*

My father doubles over in laughter.
Right now? I think.
Just when my mom
is so close.
But I have to help.
Okay, I yell.

> *THANK YOU.*

And she lowers Buddy down,
tongue flapping.
When he's almost at the bottom,
he leaps out onto me.
I reach into the basket,
take out the plastic bag inside,
hook on his leash.

> *Go on, my father says,*
> *we'll be upstairs*
> *when you get back.*

Mom

Everywhere
people are fixing things
in window frames,
carrying boxes, sweeping,
and talking on the street,
the air thick with stories and tears.

We run across to the park,
step over the broken sidewalk
where I felt the first shake;
the cement is broken
in deep cracks.
The park is full of people,
blankets spread out
like a large patchwork quilt
across the grass.
Kids play in the bright sunshine.
                    It feels normal.
I take Buddy to the trees,
where he sniffs with all his might,
and we wander in the tree line
under twisty branches,
my mind wandering into the woods.

   Etan?

I hear my name.
It sounds like my own voice
or a word far away
or maybe, I think,
it's the trees
talking to me at last.

   Etan?

It's behind me.
I look,
        then I see
                she's there,
long black hair
and bright sunlight
pouring through
her spirally curls.

Mom?

Buddy looks up,
and in one breath
I am in her arms.
She smells like
our apartment
and green apple shampoo.
Her body shakes.
        She's crying,
and I get nervous
because sometimes crying
like this used to mean
that she was really sad.
But when I pull away to look,
her face is a smile,
        she's laughing.
                She wipes her eyes
                        on her sleeve.

I couldn't wait to see you. She pulls me tighter.
Mom, I say, *we were in the community center and . . .*
I know, she says. *I heard all about it.*

We freeze in time talking without words.
　　C'mon, I brought us a whole carton of ice cream,
　　you can tell me all about it inside.

We wander home
talking about Malia and her singing,
and about how I caught a baseball
but nobody saw it.

Then, in the far corner of the playground
at the very top of the slide,
I see ballerina girl
standing with her arms
raised over her head,
Blankie tied around her neck
like a cape.
She launches down the slide
and into the arms of her mom.

Small Gifts

At the apartment we eat bagels
with lox and cream cheese.
My father takes a huge bite,
talks with his mouth full.
>   *It's going to get really busy.*
>   *But we will need to start*
>   *with our own building.*
>   *I was thinking, Etan,*
>   *that maybe some of the kids*
>   *in your school might want a little job*
>   *a few hours after school,*
>   *cleaning up, helping out?*
>   *I could pay them ten bucks a day?*
I nod, look at my mom,
and when she nods back
I feel the filling up
          of a space
                    that's been empty.

After we eat,
I go to organize my own room.
My box of *Star Wars* figurines
spilled off the shelf,
and my comic books are mixed
in a pile, some flipped all the way over.
Drawings floated to the ground,
dots of tape
still stuck
to the wall.

Etan. Mom comes in.
      She sits at the edge of my unmade bed
                 and smooths the blanket. *Sit?*
She hands me a small, thin package
covered in newspaper.
      Sorry, I didn't have time to wrap it.
I weigh it in my hands.
A spiral bound notebook,
the kind with thick paper
and a hard cover like a real book.
      I love that you kept our notebook
      with you all the time.
      It reminded me of how much love
      there is for me in the world.
I realize how much I want
to ask her the question,
         how much I don't.
I flip the notebook cover
back and forth between my fingers.
      Mom,
         are you
            going to
               stay?
Her body shifts, and she wipes her eyes.
      Yes. I'm staying, Etan. I'm here now.
      May I? and she takes the notebook,
opens to where a paper is slipped inside,
and pulls it out.

My picture of the river.
> *I think we can add all new stuff,*
> *but this one is my favorite,*
> *the blues and greens, the river of words*
> *flowing down all the time.*
> *Have your words come back, Etan?*
> *I think mine have.*
> *Maybe we don't have to be afraid anymore.*
> *Rivers are constantly being refilled*
> *and new water comes just as the old*
> *water floats away to the sea.*

Then she looks at me.
> *Sorry I'm so serious all the time.*
That's okay, I say.
> I missed it so much.
>> I missed you so much, I want to say.
> *Well, how about this?* she says.
>> *Do you know where fish keep their money?*
> I look at her confused, she's already smiling.
>> *Innnn river banks.*
I try not to laugh.
She's told me this joke
so many times.
Then we kneel down
> and clean up the action figures
>> and markers,
>>> laughing the whole time.

Rebuilding

Big trucks roll through town
with spools of wire,
long pieces of wood, metal pipes;
men and women with hard hats
chatter through walkie-talkies.
My father makes lists.

– *Mr. Cohen's bakery needs the windows reinforced.*
– *Mrs. Li needs the frame of her shop built back up.*
– *The school needs windows replaced.*
– *Mrs. Hershkowitz needs new bookshelves.*
– *The kitchen needs rewiring.*

We're building the town again,
　　　　making everything new,
　　　　　　everyone working together.

A Gift and a Promise

I stop at Mr. Cohen's bakery,
get a bagel and coffee for my grandfather.
I pause in the alley
to see all the names of the *Calypso.*
I take a napkin from the bag,
clean the dust out of the initials,
tiny patterns in the brick.

My grandfather is at his workbench
like always. Only this time,
instead of fixing something
             he is sorting
                   through the treasure box.
Oy, good. You're here.
     Good morning, Grandpa.
You are cheery today. Good!
Lots to be happy about these days, right?
When something bad happens,
even an earthquake,
it's a chance for a real miracle to happen.

     I look at him.
       We get to see what we are made of?
Exactly!
He sorts through the box,
a frame,
     an old photo,
        a silver chain
     on one side,
the empty jar of clay from the Vltava River,
       the knife,
          more colored stones
on the other side.

Slowly he slides this pile
toward me.
   Really? I ask.
Yes, he says. *You are almost thirteen,*
you should have some of these things,
but I have one condition.
Go back to synagogue.
Spend time with Rabbi Rosenthal.

I nod, take the knife from the sheath,
hold it against the light.
Then I hold the jar of clay;
it's lighter than the jar
that held the clay
from the Dead Sea.
I weigh it in my hand.
It's old, he begins, *much older than anything else.*
An artifact of our family,
something you should have now.
   Do you think if I mix it with the clay
   in the pool
   I could make a golem?
There's not enough clay in there to make a golem.
Besides, Etan, I'm not sure the golem
has a place in this world anymore.
Still, having this will always connect
you to the old world
like a bridge, to remind you
of where you came from
and who you are,
   and that anything is possible.

I close my hand around it.
I've held on to it for too long, he says,
like the shape of a memory long gone by.
But now I know.

       What, Grandpa?
He looks through the window,
down at his coffee,
back at the photograph of the *Calypso*.
He holds one of the photos from the box.
It's the people.
They are what connect us.
The things we do
      and remember together
            that matter most.   *Not the clay.*
And that's when I have an idea,
      and I know I have to tell Malia
            right away.

Back to the Forest Path

I grab an old backpack
with the treasures
from my grandfather
and set out for Malia's house.

It feels good to ride up Forest Road.
My legs feel strong.
I see families outside
beneath redwoods,
the occasional truck
on the road clearing
fallen branches.
The dragon mailbox is there,
and I coast into the driveway,
empty of cars.
No shoes—just collapsed
broken boards, piled together.

Malia's window is boarded up
with a big X made out of tape,
and the X is there on other broken boards
and parts of the house.
I know from my father
that these are the places
they need to fix first.

I go around to the back door.
    Knock, but no answer.
Where could she be?

Near the forest path
at the edge of her yard
the redwood branches
bend in the breeze.
At first I hear the quiet creak
of the bending branches,
then something else—
a voice, a song,
        the trees are talking to me!
But the song sounds familiar.
It's "Time After Time."

The Song

I run down the path;
Malia's song flitters
through the trees,
and finally I see the pool,
and the Sitting Stones,
and I notice that Malia
is not alone.

Concert

Malia stands on top
of one of the stones.
She's holding a stick
like a microphone,
and she's wearing her pink Jem wig.
She's singing with all heart,
because on another Sitting Stone
        is Lola.
Her body sways back and forth,
her hands full of tissues,
a private concert just for her.

I wait until the song fades
and clap from the path.

Really Okay

Etan! Malia leaps off the stone
and hugs me so hard
it actually hurts.
Lola couldn't come to the show,
so I wanted to give her
a real concert.
Malia scratches the skin
on her neck
and her arms the whole time.
I can't help but look.
What are you staring at? She smiles,
punches my shoulder.
     Sorry, I say.
It's okay, Etan, it comes and goes.
I'm really okay right now.

My cousins in the city
said that their whole building
was swaying just like this,
and that EVERYTHING came off their walls.
My parents are working overtime,
my dad is in Santa Cruz,
and my mom is in the city.
They say the hospitals are overflowing,
that lots of people
were hurt in the earthquake.

I look at her, nod,
but I can't contain it.
My mom is back.
She stops swaying,
stops scratching,
and hugs me tight.
Lola looks over.

Unearthing

Lola hugs us both,
then makes her way up the path.
Malia takes off the Jem wig,
closes her eyes, takes a deep breath, lets it out.
> *I like fall so much*, she says.
> *Cooler air helps my skin.*
> *Sometimes my parents*
> *say we should move to Hawaii.*
> *Lola says the Philippines,*
> *anywhere with trade winds*
> *where there's water in the air.*

I reach into my backpack,
pull out the jar of clay.
> *That one is way darker!* Malia points to the jar.

This one is from Prague.
It held the clay
that made the golem.
Malia's eyes get wide.
> *Do you have clay for everything?*

There's not enough here.
Actually, when my dad was
a kid, some other kids
were bothering him,
calling him mean names
because he is Jewish
and my grandparents weren't
from America.
> She squints her eyes. *I know all about that.*

My dad was so mad, he took the clay
from my grandfather's box
and he tried to say the right prayers
and make the golem
like in all the stories.

Malia gulps,   looks around.
    Did it? You know?

No, I say. *Well, he made it,*
but then it rained,
and all the clay washed down
and drained out to the sea.

She walks over and lifts the jar
out of my hand.
She just undoes the metal latch
            on the top
                    and the air escapes with a *POP*.

We both try to look into the jar;
we almost bonk our heads.
We hold it in the light
but we can't see anything.
        We smell it,
                and it's the smell
                        of the earth,
something familiar
        but far away,
                like a good smell on the wind
                        that is there and gone again,
                        like an earthquake.

Mix

Malia dips her finger in.
What if we mix it? she says.
I mean, what if we just take
the clay from the pool,
pour some of it into the jar,
say all the stuff?
          I don't think you can just do that, I say.
Why not?
          I don't know. You just . . . I mean . . .
But why not. Isn't that the point? she persists.
We walk over to the pool,
kneel down,
          and Malia cups water in her hands,
                    lets it fall gently into the jar.
                              Like it's some kind of ceremony.

C'mon, little golem,
if you can hear me,
come out and be free.
The sound of her voice
is like every ounce of this is true.

When the jar is full, we look at it.
Full of water, perfectly still,
a tiny reservoir at the top.

What do we do now? she asks.
          Well, I say, *if we were making a real golem,*
          we would need to place a prayer inside it,
          and then we would give it a mission.
No problem! I've got it!

She walks over to my backpack,
finds a pencil and paper,
looks at the trees,
feels some dirt between her fingers,
quickly scribbles something down.
Here's the prayer.
I take the paper,
roll it into a tiny scroll,
slip it into the jar.
    Now . . . we need a mission.
We think for a while,
I know, says Malia.
Little golem, can you find
Etan's important green rock
and bring it back to us?
I laugh. *My bareket?*
It would be nice
to have that again.

The Last of the Clay

We tilt the jar together,
let it spill out into the pool,
mostly mud-colored water
with some clay mixed in,
making ripples on the surface.
Clouds of clay
burst in the water
and slowly sink away.

The Empty Jar

It's still a rad jar, she says.
What will you do with it?
    I don't know.
    Maybe I can keep some clay from here?
    Maybe since we've mixed
    so much together
    all of it is magical now?

Malia reaches into the water,
away from where
it starts to flow into a stream,
comes back with a handful
of goopy mud.
    We pry it off her hand into the jar,
        then close the latch.

Her Idea

Malia scratches her neck
while we walk back up.
*You know, I think I'm
going to try going back to school.*

I stop.

*Don't look so surprised.
I can't stay home forever.*
She scratches her arm,
and I notice her eye
just a bit puffed out.
*It's okay, Etan, my mom always
says one day at a time,
and I think I finally believe her.*

*I can do it.
        I really can,
                and besides . . .*

We keep walking.
Besides what? I say.
She looks at me, rolls her eyes.
        I have at least one friend now.

In the Kitchen

The small TV blares
one news story after another
about "efforts to get thing back on track."
Lola gives us a plate of pancit.

So I have this idea, I say.
Malia puts her hands on her chin
like a cartoon character.
*Well, we used to have Shabbat dinner
every week, and lots of* Calypso *people
used to come, lots of other friends.*
    But we stopped when my mom got . . . well you know . . .
Malia eases up her cartoon face
                and scoops up some noodles.

*I thought we could have it again,
and this time you could come
with your family.*
                Like a reset?
*Yes, and I thought we could
start off by surprising my grandfather?*

        I LOVE IT!
Lola shouts, startling us.
She's smiling.
*It's time we all get together again.
The old and the new!*

Putting Things Back Together

Over the next week,
we learn about all the little miracles.
> *The real wonder is the bridge,*
> Mr. Cohen says.
> *It was rush hour,*
> *it should have been packed,*
> *but everyone was at the game instead.*
> *Baseball saved everyone.*

My father makes plans
to repair Malia's house
and the community center.
I go everywhere with him
like an assistant,
the front seat of his truck
filled with blueprints and lists.
> We get ice cream all the time.

My grandfather sometimes comes,
repairing the metal work,
> fastening hinges,
> all the detailed work
> that's so hard to do.

And every night,
my mother tells us about how they
are rebuilding the city.
I tell her about Malia starting school
after winter break.
I tell her about my Shabbat idea
and that we want to surprise Grandpa.
> *Of course!* she says.

Back to School

We go back on Friday
just a half day,
maybe to see
if we are okay being back.
I try to picture Malia
in the classroom, sitting in one of these desks.
Will she be okay?
She's going to make everyone laugh.

Mr. Potts lets us talk
about the earthquake;
we can talk or write about our feelings,
and that's what we do all day.
Some kids tell stories
        about hiding,
some kids talk
        about what they saw on TV . . .
and then something unexpected happens.
        I raise my hand.
I WANT to talk about it.
I talk about the talent show,
and the plaster coming down,
and my grandfather.
When I finish and look around,
I remember that I haven't said anything
out loud in a long, long time.
Maybe nobody remembers my voice.
I talk about Buddy finding us,
        and then I look at Jordan,
                and Martin, and that's when it happens.

Martin stands up, starts talking about
how we had to move heavy shelves
so Mrs. Hershkowitz could stand.
*We had to all do it together
just to get it to budge*, he says.

I look at Jordan, fidgeting in his seat,
getting ready to tell his parts of the story, too.

At Recess

Martin puts a hand on my shoulder,
    Baseball?
I look for words hiding in my gut
but they aren't there anymore.
Okay, I say,
    and Jordan hands
        me his mitt.

Synagogue

Rabbi Rosenthal
hugs all of us,
and he's not a hugger.
Then he hands
    me a folder
        full of work
            I have missed.
                See you next week? he says.
I smile.
He will, my grandfather says.
I will make sure.

World Series Returns

Game 3 finally happens.
It's one of the biggest crowds
ever at Candlestick Park.
The fans are a little quiet,
we are quiet, too,
from our living room.
Everything's changed just a bit;
baseball seems
a little further away.
My father wears his Maldonado jersey,
my mother wears his Giants cap.
The game goes fast,
and by the end of the eighth inning,
      the A's are up by 10;
even though the Giants come back
in the ninth a little bit,
      the loss makes my father quiet.

When the A's close them out in Game 4,
my father seems so tired.
I look at him.
     I guess we know what the Giants are made of now.
My father stares,
puts his arm around me.
You know what?
Imagine what it must be like,
after everything that happened,
just to show up. I mean the earth shook,
and just a few days later,
they played baseball again.
I guess that's not all that bad,
just to make it there at all.

Ancient Mysteries

On a Monday
    after school,
        I ride my bike to Malia's house,
           and we go down to the Sitting Stones
with a pile of paper
        and a bag of markers.
We spread out a blanket
        and write secret invitations for Shabbat.

It's nothing fancy,
a few words and a heart.
Do you think they will all come? she asks.
    I think so, I say.
    I hope.
    My mom is calling everyone,
    telling them not to tell my grandfather,
    but she thought it would be good
    to write these little notes
    to let everyone know that it's back on again.
After a while, we take a break.
Malia stretches her legs, sings a bit,
dances around the pool,
and I sketch in my new notebook.
Will both your parents come?
Malia?

But she doesn't answer.
Malia?
She's standing at the pool,
    her mouth open,
        finger pointing.

I run over to where she is,
and I start pointing, too,
because there,
        on the quiet shore,
            half-buried,
                is a green stone.
                        It's my bareket.
I walk over,
        reach down
            to pick it up,
but Malia grabs my hand,
        Wait! She points to tiny tracks
in the mud, smudges, like rabbit paws,
            rounded little impressions.
She looks at me in the eyes.
Do you think?
I don't say anything,
just reach down
and pick up the stone.
It fits perfectly in my hand.

We look at the pool
        and across it
            into the depths of forest,
                both of us looking for something
                        we hope is real.

The Shop

On the way down to the shop,
I notice there are still
so many cracks in the concrete,
    bits of glass
        along the side of the road,
            but things are getting better
                little by little.
I drop invitations to Mr. Dimitri
and Mr. Cohen and Mrs. Li.

In the shop
my grandfather is cleaning
his tools, wiping them
with an old rag
that smells like castor oil.

Grandpa, I need to show you something.
    I pull out the bareket,
        hold it in the center of my palm.
    I thought it was lost?
We found it.
Well, sort of.
It kind of found us?
He smiles.

Life is a mystery, isn't it?
You think you know everything,
but it's mystery that makes us human.
That forest you go to, this stone,
all the way back to the Calypso,
          the Dead Sea,
                    Prague,
and even before that.
                    Don't forget what this feels like.
                    Don't ever lose your sense of wonder.
He squeezes my shoulders with his giant hands
like he's pressing the words into me.
Then, all at once, I put my hands
on his shoulders and squeeze right back.

Shabbat

C'mon, Grandpa, it will be sunset soon!
Alright, Etan, all right. He coughs, puts on his coat,
and we walk together away from Main Street
to our apartment building,
        up the stairs,
              down the hall.
                    I hold my grandfather's hand
                       and open the door.

SURPRISE!

I feel his hand squeeze mine.
All around the table
are the faces of everyone we know,
the apartment packed,
   the air filled
      with all the voices,
          smiles, and songs.
The table is laden with tinfoiled boxes of chocolate,
silver candlesticks,
baskets full of challah
and pandesal,
bowls of gefilte fish,
bowls of steaming rice,
dishes full of adobo,
platters piled with lumpia
circling around rich, red sauces;
      steam rises from pans
full of brisket and vegetables,
Crock-Pots of corn soup,
and shining bowls of honey carrots.

Behind the table,
        in tall chairs,
                My mom and dad,
Mr. Cohen, Mrs. Li, Mr. Dimitri, Mrs. Hershkowitz,
        and Lola,
and all around them their children,
        their grandchildren,
talking and playing.
Mr. and Mrs. Agbayani beam
in fancy clothes,
        and there, between them,
                I see Malia,
in a purple dress,
        a flower in her hair,
                and a long, red scarf
                        wrapped all the way up
                                and over her eye.
She pulls me over,
        hugs me,
                then smiling,
                        she punches my shoulder,
whispers, *We did it.*
I smile.
She leans over.
        See you tomorrow
                at the Sitting Stones?
Yes, I say,
        right after synagogue!

Unexpected Guests

My father takes Grandpa's hand,
    walks him to a chair
        right next to Mrs. Li.
        He tries to talk
        but Mrs. Li doesn't let him
        because Jordan is at the door,
        standing there with his mom and dad.
            For a moment everyone stares,
            but my father walks over,
            embraces them, says words
            no one else can hear.

Jordan walks over to us,
holds up a blue binder
with a Giants sticker on the front.
I brought my cards!

Blessings

And all at once,
we feel a sudden shift in the light,
the sun moves behind the mountains
                    and the ocean beyond.
My mom raises her arm,
and everyone finds a seat,
        little kids on the floor like it's a picnic,
Me, Malia, and Jordan
        at a small card table.

Mom lights the candles,
        looks around,
                her face bright
                    in the warm glow.
She covers her eyes
        and recites the blessings;
                everyone joins in
                    the best they can.

The old and the new mix together,

making something
    completely new,
        making something
                together.

Author's Note

Just after 5 P.M. on October 17, 1989, the San Andreas Fault slipped, and Loma Prieta Peak in the Santa Cruz Mountains south of San Francisco became the epicenter of a magnitude 6.9 earthquake that lasted an astonishing fifteen seconds. It tore many parts of the Bay Area apart and damaged transportation infrastructure, including the top span of the Bay Bridge, which collapsed. The earthquake took place during Game 3 of the 1989 World Series between the San Francisco Giants and the Oakland A's. Everyone was at the game or tuning in, so the earthquake was seen all over the world—with live footage from the Goodyear Blimp. The earthquake was devastating, but it showcased the courage, resilience, and humanity of the people of the Bay Area, who came together during the crisis.

Years before the earthquake, as a seventh grader living in the Bay Area, I didn't understand earthquakes. I was afraid of them. From the very first drill, during which I had to dive under my desk, to the first time I felt the ground shake, I remember thinking that the world was being unmade. *The Magical Imperfect* recalls those times, and how at a time of personal challenge and upheaval, when even the earth is not safe, healing and hope can come from surprising places.

The fictional town of Ship's Haven, like many of the towns in the southern San Francisco area, was founded by immigrants dating back to the gold rush. In the story, the town received an even greater influx during a newer wave of immigration. This was a time when most second-generation children of immigrants commuted to larger cities for work, while many of first-generation immigrants and refugees formed tighter communities and smaller businesses to survive.

Many of these immigrants came through Angel Island. The Angel Island Immigration Station was put into operation in 1910. It became widely known as the "Ellis Island of the West." The immigrants to the United States mainly arrived there from China and Japan, but also from the Punjab, Russia, the Philippines, Portugal, Australia, New Zealand, Mexico, and Latin America, as well. It is important to note the historical and deeply complex challenges that faced the many Chinese immigrants who came via Angel Island, dealing with a range of issues, including the Chinese Exclusion Act of 1882 and various others that severely limited immigration all the way until 1965. However, many other immigrants came to Angel Island from Russia and the Philippines, and among these immigrants were several hundred Jews, fleeing Nazi rule in Germany, Austria, Poland, Hungary, and Czechoslovakia. Different groups of immigrants were treated differently. A stunning and comprehensive history of Angel Island immigration can be found in the landmark book *Angel Island: Immigrant Gateway to America* by Erika Lee and Judy Yung (New York: Oxford University Press, 2010).

While there are a few stories about Jews who successfully made it, there are many more stories that are not well documented and are waiting to be discovered.

Angel Island became a California State Park by 1963.

The story of Etan's grandfather is fictionalized, but his story is based on one of many Jewish refugees who came from Europe on those last ships. It also tells the story of Malia's family, immigrants from the Philippines. These are important connections for my family—my own Jewish background and also the Filipino side of my family—from which so many stories are waiting to be told.

Malia has severe atopic dermatitis, also known as eczema, a skin condition that causes rashes that itch and swollen, dry, and scaly skin that can cover your entire body and can cause depression, isolation, and immeasurable discomfort. My wife, who is also a Filipina, has had to work through her eczema for most of her life and all of our married life. It is something that our family struggles, learns, and loves our way through almost every day.

I hope that this book lights the way for others to come to a better understanding of conditions like eczema, and that it will help others find compassion and perhaps even hope. Just like the characters in the book, no matter who we are or where we come from, we can all experience the healing power (and magic) of friendship and love.

Acknowledgments

Nothing could be more magically imperfect than trying to thank everyone who has been a part of the creation of this book.

I am profoundly grateful for my amazing agent, Rena Rossner, for always believing in me and for soul searching with me to help the drafts of this book form into the story it needed to be. Thank you to the incredible Liz Szabla for the extraordinary vision for this story, for generosity, and for tireless work. Thank you for believing in Etan and Malia, and for always honoring me as a writer. It is a privilege (and lots of fun) to work with you. Thanks to the whole team at Feiwel and Friends: Dawn Ryan, Executive Managing Editor; Kathy Wielgosz, Production Editor; Trisha Previte, Associate Designer; and publicist Kelsey Marrujo. A huge thanks to the amazing cover artist, André Ceolin, for perfectly capturing the magical spirit of the book! Of course, thank you to Jean Feiwel for your warmth and your vision, and for making me feel so at home at F&F.

Thank you to the teachers, librarians, and educators who put books in the hands of kids who need them and for standing up for *all* children every day no matter who they are.

Thanks to my foundational people in the SDSU MFA program, who took this college athlete and showed him that it was okay to be multidimensional. Thank you for believing in me as a writer even though it took some time. Sandra Alcosser, Marilyn Chin, Glover Davis, and so many others. Thank you to my colleagues and students at San Diego City College and, of course, the English Center.

An unending thanks to my people, my community who supports

me through it all, whether it's lending an ear, planting trees, or reading manuscripts. Thank you for being family. Matt and Caroline de la Peña; Heather Eudy; Cali Linfor; Sabrina Youmans; Virginia Loh-Hagan; Jeannie Celestial; Rena's Renegades; the JPST: Rajani LaRocca, Josh Levy, Jessica Kasper Kramer, Nicole Panteleakos, Cory Campbell Leonardo, Naomi Milliner, and Gillian McDunn. Thanks to Dan Haring, Chris Tebbets, Jarret Lerner, Sally J. Pla, and Mae Respicio for always supporting me and helping me to be the best writer I can be. And thanks to the unbelievable world of middle grade and YA authors who care so much for kids and one another. You bring me so much hope. Thank you for your friendship.

Thank you to all the wise sages in my life: Nick; Maggie; Emmett; Chris; my brother, Steve; the Tuesday Morning crew; WellSpring; and so many others who keep me on the right path and help me remember where I come from.

Thank you to the Rosensweigs, who many years ago made the long trip and came through Ellis Island to start a new life. We owe you everything.

Thanks to my mother, the artist, who always teaches me—even now—to always do the work. Thank you for believing that anything is possible, and for teaching me that art can save the world.

Maraming salamat to my Filipino family who has loved me without fail since I first "towered over everyone": Phillip, Elise, Christiana, and Savannah Dizon. Thank you to Lola: Emelita DeCastro-Vega for always loving me as a son.

Thank you to my son, Asa, and my daughters, Samaria and Caylao, for healing me, and filling my life with fun and joy I can't measure. You are my favorite human beings. Thank you for being so understanding during all the times that I had to "WRITE A BOOK."

And most of all, thank you to my brilliantly creative, openhearted, beautiful and unstoppable wife, Ella, for her unconditional love and support for me, for this book, and for this life we are building together.

Lastly, thank you to all the readers out there. I hope you enjoyed *The Magical Imperfect*. I hope that Etan and Malia's story inspires you to be fearless, dream big, work hard, and find the magic in your life. Always be hopeful. The world needs you just the way you are.